Here comes the bride . . .

Jamie realized she was trembling. She pressed back against Drew and felt his arms go around her. It comforted her. A little.

Then Jamie saw it.

A shimmering figure high above the crowd, hovering there like a flaming angel.

An avenging angel, thought Jamie irrelevantly.

"Drew," she managed to say. "Do you see her?"

"Yes," answered Drew, softly.

It was the bride. The ghostly bride.

Someone else looked and saw the apparition. Someone else screamed what Jamie had only thought.

"It's her! She's come back for revenge. She's going to kill us all! It's the bride!"

Then, suddenly, the lights came on.

And the bride was gone. . . .

Also by D. E. Athkins:

The Ripper
Sister Dearest
Mirror, Mirror

THE BRIDE

D. E. ATHKINS

SCHOLASTIC INC.
New York Toronto London Auckland Sydney

ISBN 0-590-25490-1

12 11 10 9 8 7 6 5 4 3 2 1   6 7 8 9/9 0 1/0

Printed in the U.S.A.   01

First Scholastic printing, June 1996

THE BRIDE

Chapter 1

So much blood. Amazing that such a little cut in the flesh could produce so much blood.

She was dark with dark hair and brown eyes and she was wearing a long, shimmering dress of pink silk. She was beautiful.

She was famous for her looks. Her very expensive looks.

And her very bad temper.

But she didn't lose her famous temper. She just stared down at the red oozing up from her hand. At the heavy silver, jeweled letter opener that pinned her hand to the table by a bead of blood and a tatter of flesh. At the pale, perfectly manicured hand that held the letter opener.

When she did look up at the triumphant, translucently pale face above hers, framed in a spill of golden hair and ivory bridal lace, her expression didn't change.

Which made it more frightening somehow.

"She's crazy!" whispered the stunned photographer's assistant to the flunky standing next to him.

"Who?" the other shot back. "The bridesmaid? Or the bride?"

"Perfect," the photographer cried, his camera clicking, clicking, clicking. "Don't move a *muscle*. Hold it . . . hold it. Outrageous, darlings, perfect, perfect, darlings!"

The bridesmaid began to laugh.

"Get a doctor!" someone shouted.

"She's hysterical," said someone else.

"Just stay calm," a professionally soothing voice broke in.

Blaine Harrod took her hand off the jeweled handle of the letter opener. "I'm *so* sorry, Alison, darling," she said. "An accident. You know?"

Alison Dewitt closed her own fingers around the handle of the letter opener. She jerked it out without even looking at her hand, or flinching.

The point had nicked the edge of her little finger.

"Accident?" she drawled, softly. She held

up the letter opener as if to admire its shining silver surface. She studied her lipstick for a moment in the flat of the wicked little blade.

Then quick as a cat she lunged across the table at her rival model.

A prop manager shrieked, "Be careful! The letter opener's an antique! It's only on loan!"

The assistants pulled them apart before any real damage was done.

All the time the photographer kept shooting and shooting and shooting, murmuring, in his faintly French-accented English, "Excellent! Brilliant! This will sell out the magazine."

In her dressing room, Blaine Harrod bent forward to study her face in the mirror. She'd always been a bad girl, a bad but beautiful girl. She'd always been a little superstitious, too, afraid, somehow, the mirror would start reflecting just how bad she was.

It had never happened before. It hadn't happened now.

She smiled at herself in the glass. She kept smiling as her assistant came in and closed the door with a disapproving thump.

Blaine's smile deepened. "Clara, would you be a saint and send Alison a dozen roses with my apologies?"

"Roses," said Clara expressionlessly. "You're pushing your luck, Blaine. Even you can go too far."

"Roses," said Blaine firmly. She added, "It really was an accident."

Her eyes met Clara's.

Blaine looked away first.

"I'll send the roses," Clara said then.

"Oh, dear," said Jamie's mother. "I don't know. A whole weekend? All by yourself?"

"There'll be a million people there, Mom. Including Blaine *and* Aunt Charlotte."

The idea of Blaine and her mother, Charlotte, didn't seem to reassure Mrs. Haroldson. She fingered the heavy, engraved invitations on the table. The one addressed to her and Jamie's father was gratifying. It was nice to know a niece had done so well, even a niece as difficult as Blaine had been.

But the separate invitation to Jamie was more troubling. Because it included a heavy sheet of paper slashed with Blaine's characteristically bold handwriting:

Jamie. Come early to the wedding and stay at Sandhill and meet everybody. Wedding rehearsal Friday night, maximum party on Saturday night, and the deed is done on Sunday

afternoon. You are *going to be one of my brides-maids, aren't you? Sordid details to follow!!!*
B.

Charlotte Blaine Haroldson (until she'd changed her name to something more exotic), Jamie's first cousin, had been gone from the little town of Point Harbor for four years. Gone but not forgotten. She was "That Haroldson Girl" still, the one who was "Not Nice."

Wild. Crazy. Bad. A sort of Pied Piper who used her beauty and compelling charm to lead their sons and daughters astray.

Too smart for her own good, Jamie's mother had always said.

Blaine hadn't cared. She'd only been marking time until she could get out of town. Way, *way* out of town. Shake off her Point Harbor past forever.

To be rich and famous.

And as bad as she wanted to be.

Blaine had left when she was seventeen, to the relief of her newly remarried mother, as well as of every other adult in town.

She hadn't been back since.

Only thirteen-year-old Jamie had missed her. Everyone else, when they thought of Blaine, hoped she'd come to the bad end she deserved.

Which made it all the more important to Jamie — and of course, to Blaine — that Blaine succeed.

Blaine had never called. She'd barely written, except to Jamie. And Jamie had hidden those letters, full of funny tales of grim apartments and cockroaches and late-night cab rides halfway home until the money ran out.

Then, overnight, everything had changed. The news had arrived on the covers of magazines, in the gossip columns. Blaine Harrod had made it.

After that, extravagant Christmas presents had replaced the Christmas cards that were all Blaine had once been able to afford to send to her family. And Jamie's presents were the best of all, which was why Jamie owned a leather skirt that was so short that she had to sneak it out of the house to wear it. And sunglasses that cost more than she earned in a month working after school in her father's hardware store.

Gifts from her bad cousin that brought the same worried look to her mother's eyes that the invitation to Blaine's wedding did now. . . .

And made Jamie's heart beat faster.

"Aunt Charlotte will keep an eye on me," said Jamie, knowing that it wasn't true, that

Blaine's mother lived in a world of her own, saving most of her attention for herself.

Jamie knew her mother knew it, too. But her mother couldn't say that about her own sister-in-law. So all she said was, "Well, we'll see."

And Jamie knew she had won.

Chapter 2

A man in a uniform was checking everybody's invitation.

Was it Jamie's imagination or did he stare at Jamie and her mother before nodding and waving them through? "Park in the front," he instructed. "The valets will see to your car."

The house wasn't visible from the gate, of course. Not until they'd driven around a small pond, in which two swans swam and preened, and through a wall of sand dunes, did the house rise before their eyes.

"Whoaa," breathed Jamie.

"I don't know about this," said Mrs. Haroldson for about the hundredth time.

Sandhill was a huge, misshapen house that looked as if it had been built by a child out of gray stone blocks and chunks of cedar. Chimneys sprouted randomly from the roof, and only later did Jamie realize that at least one of the enormous chimneys was in fact a turret. Leaded windows glinted in the sun. The house seemed to sprawl in every direction.

Before it had been sold by feuding heirs, Sandhill had once been the biggest summer home among the summer home estates of the wealthy that nestled in the dunes near the ocean. Most of the summer homes were practically big enough to put the whole town of Point Harbor in. And many of the people in Point Harbor worked for those same people, including, indirectly, Jamie's mother and father, who ran the nearest hardware store.

Although Sandhill was only a few miles from Point Harbor, it might as well have been the other side of the moon.

Neither Jamie nor her mother spoke again until they had stopped in the courtyard in front of the house. Mrs. Haroldson edged the battered station wagon in among the rows of gleaming Benzes, Jags, and BMWs that had preceded it, and pulled to a stop. The car looked as out of place as Jamie felt.

The people getting out of other cars all wore dark glasses and perfect clothes and smiled perfect smiles with perfect teeth. Everyone looked self-confident. As if they owned the world.

Maybe they did, thought Jamie. Maybe Blaine was right.

And then she thought, *I don't belong here.*

Yes, I do, she thought. *I have the dark glasses. And the attitude.* She reached up to touch the dark glasses that had been a birthday gift from Blaine and was comforted. A little.

Another man in a uniform motioned them forward and leaped to open the door on the driver's side. "I'll park this for you, ma'am," he offered.

"I'm not staying," said Mrs. Haroldson, waving the valet away.

Jamie took a deep breath.

Her mother's hand closed over her wrist. "I want you to have a good time, Jamie," she said. "But don't let all this go to your head."

"Mother, *puh-lease*! I know I'm not ever going to be beautiful and famous like Blaine, okay?"

"You're beautiful to me," said her mother.

Jamie rolled her eyes. Her mother was so from another planet sometimes. "See you guys at the wedding," she said and ducked quickly out of the car, grabbing her suitcase from the backseat.

"Darling, you made it!"

Jamie looked up. Blinked.

Blaine was standing there, on the bottom

step of the stairs leading up into Sandhill. Blaine as she had always been. And yet, somehow, changed. . . .

Well, what did you expect after four years? Jamie asked herself.

Turning, Blaine said to the quiet, almost mousy woman standing next to her, "Clara, make sure this gets up to Jamie's room."

"Clara, hi!" Jamie extended her hand. "We've talked on the phone about the wedding plans. Remember?"

"Ah. Of course. You haven't met. I've talked to Clara so much about you, Jamie, that I feel as if you had. Clara, my cousin, Jamie, as you must already know. There. You've been officially introduced. I couldn't live without Clara, you know. Without Clara, my address would be the lost and found."

"You sound like a country music song," said Clara. Jamie was surprised. Clara's quick comeback didn't go with her quiet appearance. Nor did the sharp brown eyes with which she peered at Jamie for a moment over the tops of her little square glasses before she reached out to give Jamie's hand a quick, businesslike shake. "How do you do?" she said formally. Then she flipped open a small leather-bound book and made a note in it.

Blaine, meanwhile, had leaned over to give

Jamie's mother a hug. "Aunt Susan," she cooed. "Thank you *so* much for letting Jamie come. She's going to have a *fabulous* time."

"Not too fabulous, I hope," said Susan Haroldson primly.

"Are you worried I'll corrupt Jamie? I'm not the bad girl of Point Harbor anymore, I promise."

In spite of herself, Mrs. Haroldson smiled. "It's good to see you, dear. We're looking forward to the wedding." She fixed a sharp eye on Jamie. "Behave," she ordered. She put the station wagon in gear and drove away.

"Wow. Aunt Susan hasn't changed. She still terrifies me."

"She never terrified you," retorted Jamie. "No one ever did."

Clara snorted. A small silence fell among the three. Then Clara cleared her throat and said, "*I* have things to attend to. Nice to meet you, Jamie."

With an imperious wave of her small hand, Clara summoned the hovering bellhop. She followed him and his pile of luggage into the hotel.

"You've grown," said Blaine. She touched Jamie's left cheek lightly. "Good bones. Hmmm. Let's see. I have to go play kiss-kiss hostess with all the guests right now. Who . . . ah! Drew! Over here!" To Jamie out of the side of her mouth, she said, "Drew's sister is one of my dear, *dear* friends. Drew's her little brother . . ."

"Someone's *little* brother!" Jamie began in protest. But Blaine had already turned away to call across the crowd, "Drew! Drew, I *need* you."

Jamie groaned inwardly.

"But do you want me?" a voice asked, laughing.

He was just a little taller than Jamie. He had long brown hair and green eyes and he was only the most gorgeous guy she'd ever seen in her life. At least, in person.

She forgot about every boy she'd ever known. In fact she forgot how to talk. She just stared.

"Drew, Jamie, my cousin, first cousin, in fact," said Blaine. "Play together nice, now, you guys. See you later." She was gone.

"Hi," said Jamie. She swallowed hard. "Uh, come here often?"

Well, that made the top ten stupid-question list of the world, she thought.

But if he thought so, Drew gave no sign. "I've never actually stayed here before. The locals think it's, oh, very slightly tacky, you know." He gestured with his hand and Jamie realized that by "locals," Drew meant the people who lived in the surrounding estates, not the people from Point Harbor. "They say it's haunted, too. Trust Blaine to have her wedding in a haunted house . . ."

"Haunted! But . . ." Jamie was going to say, *but I've lived around here all my life and I've never heard of any ghost.* She stopped. No. Aloud she said, "But you don't believe in ghosts, do you?"

Drew shrugged. "Get this," he said. "It's the ghost of a bride."

"No way," said Jamie.

Before she could ask him anything else, Drew had caught her hand and turned. "Come on," he said. He led the way up the stairs to the front door of Sandhill, nodding to the people as he passed.

Jamie saw faces she'd only seen in magazines and newspapers. She tried not to stare.

She concentrated on staring at Drew out of the corner of her eye.

When they'd almost reached the top of the stairs, a slender, strong-looking girl in a pale green, clinging jumpsuit detached herself from a small group of people and said, "Drew!"

"Kel," he said, kissing her lightly on the cheek.

Kelly turned her huge, sparkling green eyes

toward Jamie expectantly. It was the face that had launched a thousand magazine covers.

"Jamie Harrod," Drew said. "My sister, Kelly Kane."

"Blaine's cousin," said Kelly instantly. "You're just like her!"

"No, I'm not!" Jamie was startled into answering. She blushed and said, "I mean, you know, thanks, but I'm dark and she's fair and . . ." Her voice trailed off.

Now they were both looking at her. Drew's eyes, Jamie noted irrelevantly, were just as green as Kelly's.

"Uh, Haroldson, actually," Jamie tried again. "My name is Jamie Haroldson. Blaine, uh, changed her last name."

"Oh, don't we all! Except Drew hasn't changed his, have you, darling brother?"

"Kaminsky born and Kaminsky bred and when I die I'll be Kaminsky dead," said Drew.

Kelly made a face. "Save your camp songs for the kiddies . . . Oh, look, Kaminsky . . . there's Preston, being all nice and charming at the door."

The only time Jamie had seen Preston Alden was in the photograph of Blaine and him in the engagement announcement in the Point Harbor newspaper.

Blaine, Jamie remembered, had always said she would only marry a man who was filthy rich and drop-dead gorgeous.

She'd kept her word. And more.

The photograph hadn't begun to do him justice.

"Wow," said Jamie. She instinctively reached up and lowered her sunglasses.

Kelly said, "You haven't met your future cousin-in-law? Then we must go do the meet and greet, darlings." She slid her arm through Jamie's and led her forward.

The closer they got, the better he looked.

He was older. He looked as if he was used to being in charge. As if he knew what he wanted and how to get it — no matter what *it* was.

Jamie blushed at the sudden thought of just what Pres might want . . .

As if he heard Jamie's thoughts, Pres suddenly turned his head in their direction. The color rushed to Jamie's face. She was glad she was wearing the sunglasses. She was glad he couldn't see her eyes.

Then Kelly was murmuring words of introduction and Pres was bending forward to shake Jamie's hand. He smiled and she felt her heart beat faster. His fingers clasped hers. Held on.

Held on for a moment longer than necessary.

His skin seemed to burn hers. Startled, she stepped back. His fingers tightened for a moment and then he released her. His smile deepened.

"Welcome to the family," he said. "Blaine didn't tell me about *you*."

"She didn't tell me about you, either," Jamie said, trying to sound unruffled.

He laughed suddenly.

Then a voice said, "Smile, dear ones."

Kelly turned automatically. Jamie looked over her shoulder.

A small, round man with a fantastic black mustache and a huge camera bobbed up in front of them.

The camera flashed.

Jamie blinked. A sea of faces turned for a moment in their direction. A giddy sensation passed over her.

Was this how Blaine lived her life now? It all seemed so fantastic. So unreal.

Then she saw her cousin down below in the crowd.

Blaine's face was turned up like a flower to the sun. But the expression on her face was anything but flowerlike. She was staring up at Jamie with narrowed, angry eyes.

Evil eyes.

Eyes filled with hatred and rage.

At that moment, Blaine had never looked more beautiful.

Or more deadly.

Chapter 3

The camera clicked.

Jamie blinked.

The photographer said, "Fabulous, darlings," and rushed away.

And Blaine was smiling again as if she never did anything but smile. She bent forward to greet another guest.

Jamie glanced quickly around. Neither Drew nor Kelly, nor Pres, for that matter, seemed to have noticed.

You're imagining things, thought Jamie. *Nerves. Blaine would never look at me like that. Not in a million years. Hey, girl, you're a bridesmaid in her wedding, remember?*

"See you at the party tonight," said Pres. He was talking to all of them. But the way he said it sounded intimate. As if he was making a special promise . . .

"See ya," said Kelly. To Jamie she said,

"Now, I must get some rest. I'm exhausted. It took me hours and *hours* to get here. From Kansas. Have you ever been to Kansas?"

Drew said, "I thought it was Nebraska."

"Flat. It was flat," said Kelly. "In *every* way . . ."

"Follow me," said Drew. "The wedding party is all on the same floor. Pretty little bridesmaids, all in a row . . ." He made a face. "And I'm in outer Siberia."

"Or Kansas," said Jamie.

Drew grinned. It was a nice smile. *Much nicer than Pres's,* Jamie thought suddenly.

But then, she didn't think Pres was very nice. She didn't think *nice* was what Pres had in mind.

Was it possible that Blaine had met her match at last?

"Darling," said Kelly, when they reached Jamie's room. "I'm right down the hall there, where I will, in five minutes, be sleeping. Deeply." She pointed. "Come down and join us before the party. We'll all go together."

Drew looked back over his shoulder as his sister dragged him away. "Later," he said.

The way he said it was a promise, too.

Casual.

What did that mean? Tonight was the wedding rehearsal in the great ballroom. And a party afterward in the small ballroom.

Casual dress, Clara had told her, going over the schedule on the phone earlier in the week.

The words "casual" and "ballroom" somehow didn't seem to go together.

Jamie sat up and yawned. As Kelly had planned on doing, Jamie had slept deeply. She hadn't meant to. She'd only meant to lie down for a minute.

She checked her watch and practically leaped from the bed. Not a minute to lose. She yawned again, frowning. She had a feeling that the Laura Ashley dress her mother had made her bring wasn't quite what Blaine and her other guests would be wearing tonight. In fact, she had a feeling that, with the exception of her bridesmaid's dress, she didn't have a thing to wear.

She looked longingly down at her black jeans.

And thought even more longingly of her black leather skirt.

Maybe I could just stay in my room, she thought. She got up and crossed to the window. The room was in shadows, but it wasn't quite dark outside. She pushed the curtain aside to stare down at the darker outlines of manicured flower beds against the grass below. Beyond she could see a ribbon of ocean in the deepening twilight. The ghostly oval of her own face was reflected back at her from the windowpane.

Look, Ma, no clothes, she thought. *And I don't think I can get by on my looks in this crowd.*

She was about to turn away when she heard it. A faint, persistent sound. Faint, muffled, horrible. Moaning. Wailing.

Dying.

It was behind her.

She froze. An unearthly cry sounded in Jamie's ears.

She turned so quickly she almost lost her balance. Clutching the curtain, she gasped, "Who-who's there?"

No one answered.

The shadows in her room had deepened into still darkness.

The lights are off and no one's here, she told herself. She stepped forward toward the lamp at the side of her bed and stopped.

For one moment, the scent of roses flooded the room.

Jamie wrinkled her nose. The odor was overwhelming. *Light first,* she thought, *and then I'm opening the window.*

She wondered if she'd have the nerve to

complain to the manager about the ventilation in her room.

Then a movement in the old-fashioned mirror on its stand in the corner caught Jamie's eye.

Jamie stopped. She blinked.

She was standing nowhere near the mirror. No way could it have caught her reflection.

Almost against her will she stepped forward.

And then Jamie saw her: a pale, old-fashioned girl, her hair pulled back, her mouth open. She was dressed all in white, lacy, glowing white. White roses spilled from her hand.

Only she wasn't standing in Jamie's room.

She was looking back at Jamie from the mirror.

Chapter 4

The ghost reached out toward Jamie. Its hand came out of the mirror, long icy fingers groping blindly, hungrily.

"N-no," stuttered Jamie, backing away.

She reached blindly behind her, trying to find the doorknob.

The ghost stepped forward. Roses spilled from her arms. Spilled from the mirror out onto the heavy, patterned carpet.

Spilled soundlessly, weightlessly, each rose lit by a pale light of its own.

The room grew cold.

Jamie's fingers found the doorknob. Fumbled.

Another hand came out of the mirror.

"No!" shrieked Jamie.

Never taking her eyes off the thing wavering in the dark mirror, she opened the door.

She slammed it behind her and ran.

The dark-wood paneled corridor was empty. Her feet made no sound on the carpet. The sound of ghostly weeping seemed to follow her. The scent of roses clung to her clothes.

Which room was Kelly's? Hardly knowing what she was doing, she pounded blindly on a door.

A tall, dark girl with short, sleek black hair answered the door. "A ghost . . . mirror . . ." Jamie gasped.

The tall girl drew back slightly, looking startled. "Excuse me?" she said, raising her eyebrows.

"Yeah, I've had days when I'd swear it was a *monster* looking back from my mirror at me," a light, quick voice said behind the tall girl. "Let her in, Alison. It's Jamie. Jamie Harrod. You know, Blaine's cousin."

The part of Jamie's mind that wasn't reeling with shock registered the fact that the girl who was staring at her in disbelief, who was reluctantly moving aside to let her in, was Alison Dewitt.

Another face that had launched a thousand magazine covers. And a thousand rumors.

Including the rumor of a feud to the death with Blaine.

Alison said sharply, "Jamie Harrod? And you

say you saw a ghost in your room?"

Jamie hurled herself forward. "I did. I did! In the mirror! I saw her, I swear it!"

Alison frowned hard at Jamie. Then she turned her back on her and strolled to a deep, overstuffed chair in one corner of the room. Sitting down, she tilted her head to one side and studied Jamie as if she were from another planet.

"Blaine's cousin? I believe she *has* mentioned you. I can see the resemblance. A little over the top, aren't we? I mean, really. A ghost!"

"Hey, take it out on Blaine, not on me," said Jamie, before she could think.

Alison raised her eyebrows again. "Ooooh," she murmured.

Kelly stopped in mid-transit from closet to bed, her arms full of clothes. "Alison, chill . . . Jamie, are you sure? You're *serious*?"

Jamie nodded violently. She suddenly realized she was shaking.

"Drink some water," Alison suggested, sounding almost bored. "You look horrible."

"Ignore Alison," Kelly ordered. "Tell, tell, tell."

Hardly knowing what she was doing, Jamie staggered over to the clothes-strewn bed and sat down. While Alison maintained a skeptical silence and Kelly continued to fling clothes everywhere in a seemingly random fashion, Jamie told them what she had seen and heard. "And this smell, it was *intense*," she concluded lamely, her voice trailing off.

She suddenly felt foolish. It sounded so absurd.

Was it possible that she had been dreaming?

"Wait," said Jamie. She held up her arm and sniffed the sleeve of her shirt. Surely some faint scent of roses still clung to her clothes? "Smell this," she said. "Can you smell that?"

Kelly obediently sniffed. But she shook her head. "Sorry."

"I'll pass on the sniff test," said Alison dryly.

"Roses," said Jamie. "It was overwhelming. From the roses she was carrying. Or maybe her perfume."

"Roses!" Kelly exclaimed, her eyes impossibly brighter. "Roses! Why didn't you say so? That proves it, then. You did see it. You saw the ghost!"

"Puh-lease," said Alison.

"What ghost?" demanded Jamie. But even as she said it, she knew. Even before Kelly answered, she knew.

"The ghost bride," said Kelly.

"Kelly, grow *up*," Alison said.

Lowering her voice dramatically, Kelly went

on. "Back when this place was built, near the turn of the century, the owner's only daughter fell in love with a gardener. He was in charge of the rose gardens, in which the daughter had a special interest. . . . Anyway, the girl's mother had arranged a marriage for her to some rich snob. When she found out her daughter was in love with the gardener, she paid him off. The gardener left.

"Then the mother locked her daughter in her room. Everyone in the big old house could hear her crying and crying all night long, night after night. But no one dared go comfort her. Then, one night, the crying stopped. When they went in, they found her there on her bed, all dressed in her wedding clothes. She was dead.

"They couldn't find a cause of death. A broken heart, everyone whispered. Anyway, her ghost still haunts Sandhill. And," Kelly lowered her voice, "her name was Rose."

Kelly's green eyes bored into Jamie's hazel ones.

"It can't be," whispered Jamie. "You're making it up."

But her voice lacked conviction and she knew it. Even as she denied Kelly's story, Jamie could see the long, pale fingers reaching out, see the glowing roses tumbling soundlessly to the carpet . . .

"I bet you are even in her *room*!" Kelly declared dramatically.

Alison broke in, "That's impossible, Kelly, and you know it. They completely redid this place when they turned it into a hotel."

"It could still be Rose's old room."

Alison stretched and yawned like a big cat. "It can't be. Where did you hear that story, anyway? I never heard a word about it."

"It's *true*," insisted Kelly.

"In fact," said Alison, "it sounds like just the sort of rumor Blaine would put around for a little extra publicity."

"Blaine wouldn't do that!" said Jamie hotly.

"Then it was a dream," said Alison. "I bet you were asleep, weren't you?"

The doubts returned. "Y-es, but . . ."

"You were probably still half asleep, dreaming. You smelled someone's perfume, from the hallway, which isn't so surprising. God knows some of these people bathe in it. And you saw a shadow." A tiny smile curled the corners of Alison's lips. "I don't know what you heard. Maybe Pres made Blaine cry. The sound of Blaine Harrod crying would be enough to frighten anyone out of their wits."

"Hey, Blaine is Jamie's cousin, okay?" interrupted Kelly. She dropped the clothes she was holding in a heap at her feet and put her hands on her hips. "You know what your problem is, Alison Dewitt? You totally lack sensitivity. Not to mention imagination!"

"Let's just say I have a good connection with reality," shot back Alison. "Like I don't believe everything everyone tells me."

Then, abruptly, she said to Jamie, "What are you wearing tonight?"

Jamie blinked at the sudden change of subject.

Alison said, "You don't have anything to wear, do you?"

"You'll have to forgive Alison," said Kelly. "She went to charm school at the discount mall."

"Do you?" repeated Alison. Then she said, beneath her breath, "Typical Blaine."

Jamie opened her mouth to protest again. But she never got a chance.

"Take it off," ordered Alison.

"What?" said Jamie.

Alison said, "Lose the wrappings, Jamie. We haven't got all day."

Losing interest in the ghost as quickly as she had seized upon it, Kelly said to Alison,

"Oh, Alison! Fabulous idea." To Jamie she said, "Don't be shy. You should see us at the runway shows. We undress in the middle of *crowds*, don't we, Alison?"

"And some of us enjoy it," said Alison, giving Kelly a look.

Kelly giggled.

"What? What are you talking about?" Jamie was totally bewildered.

"Here," said Kelly, throwing a cashmere sweater in Jamie's direction. "Try this on. We're going to lend you some rags."

"But . . ."

"We haven't got all night, okay?" said Alison.

Jamie shrugged. "Okay," she said, trying to act as if it were no big deal. She squirmed out of her sweater and jeans and began to pull on the clothes that seemed to be hurled at her from all directions.

A few minutes later, Jamie was almost ready to believe that the ghost *had* been a dream. After all, she had been asleep. And the room had been dark. And the house was an old one.

This, she thought, allowing herself to be utterly seduced by the silks and cashmeres, the gauze and shimmer of the rich materials and famous names on the clothes that were being flung in her direction, *this is real.*

Or maybe this was the dream. If it was, she never wanted to wake up.

"You guys brought all this for the weekend?" asked Jamie as Kelly dumped more clothes on top of the pile on the bed.

"Of course," said Kelly, coming into Alison's room through the connecting door with another armload of clothes. "Why?"

"No reason," said Jamie quickly.

Under Kelly and Alison's guidance, Jamie tried on sweaters, dresses, skirts, pants, and jumpsuits. At last Alison narrowed her eyes and leaned back in her chair.

"Fabulous," Kelly gushed. "We are geniuses, aren't we, Alison?"

Alison said, "It helps to have something to work with."

Jamie looked at Alison. Was that a compliment?

"You do have good bones," said Kelly. "The Harrod family cheekbones, I guess. However, don't forget that I contributed the sweater."

Jamie didn't bother to correct Kelly about the "Harrod" family cheekbones. She just stared at herself in the mirror. A stranger stared back, a tall, lean stranger in velvet pants and a cropped cashmere top woven with sparkling thread. Alison had pulled Jamie's unruly dark hair back. Now she stood up and slipped one of the elastic rhinestone bracelets off her arm. She slipped the bracelet onto Jamie's hair at the nape of her neck, holding the hair in place.

"That's even better," Alison said. "Come on, let's go play members of the wedding. And then we party."

"Seriously." Kelly giggled. "Stick with us, Jamie. It's going to be a wild night!"

Chapter 5

It was a soaring glitter dome of chandeliers and mirrors, of light and reflection. The first rows of chairs had already been set out for the wedding on either side of deep red carpet that led from the great entry doors to a small, low stage at the far end of the room. Above the center of the stage hung a white satin canopy. A swarm of activity filled the place. Kelly and Alison were unmoved by it all, but Jamie stopped in the doorway to stare.

"The stage will be the altar — filled with flowers, of course," said a voice next to Jamie. "Rumor has it that pairs of doves are going to be hidden behind the canopy and released at the end of the ceremony."

"I hope they're house-trained," said Jamie, turning to smile at Drew.

Clara bustled up, a busy, small intense mouse. She was holding a handful of roses.

"Here," she said, thrusting a rose at Jamie. "Stay right there."

She hurried away to hustle Kelly and Alison back to the door. "The bridesmaids are supposed to wait on the other side of this entrance door. . . ." She gave Drew a frowning look and he laughed.

"You got me," he said. "I'm not a bridesmaid. I'm not even a member of the wedding. I just like to watch."

Clara said, "We haven't got much time."

"I'm going, I'm going," said Drew. He gave Jamie an exaggerated wink and said, "Party on."

Jamie, Kelly, and Alison allowed Clara to herd them back into the corridor which led from the main wing of the hotel.

"The party's going to be in the *small* ballroom," said Alison, her tone faintly derisive. "That would be the little room, no bigger than your average castle, down the hall there."

Jamie nodded, trying to appear as unimpressed by it all as Kelly and Alison were.

A small, dark, vivacious girl who looked a little younger than Jamie cannoned up to them. She flung herself so hard into one of the delicate-looking, brocaded chairs lining the hallway that it rocked back.

"Super!" she cried. "Isn't this all too super!"

Alison sat down in one of the chairs next to her, leaned back, closed her eyes and drawled, "Wake me when it's over."

The girl laughed, completely unfazed by Alison's near-rudeness. "It's true. No one cares *what* the bridesmaids do. We could walk down the aisles backwards and naked and everyone would still be watching for the bride. I don't know why we have to rehearse at all. . . ."

Before anyone could respond, Clara reappeared, her book open. "Kelly, Alison, Jamie . . . Stephanie Alden, good, there you are . . ." she said to the vivid, dark-haired girl. She frowned. "But we're missing a bridesmaid. Where's Patricia Anne? Has anyone seen Patricia Anne Thomas? She should be here."

Stephanie giggled. "Hell hath no fury like an ex-girlfriend. She was Mummy and Daddy's chosen one from the cradle, you know. She's related to us, you know. Keep the money and all that blue, blue blood in the family. All the while that Pres dated the fast and the fabulous, she waited patiently for him to come back to her and do the right thing." Stephanie put her hand up to her mouth and giggled again. "But then Pres met Blaine. A model. Mums was furious. She *hates* publicity of any kind! Nothing makes her warp out faster. And all the gossip! Especially after everyone had been saying he was going to marry Pats. Poor Patricia never had a chance . . ."

"How crude you are, Stephanie. No doubt when you've outgrown your terrible teens you'll improve," said a cold voice.

With a yelp, Stephanie almost levitated out of her chair. "Patricia!"

Jamie's eyes widened. Beside her she heard Kelly stifle a giggle. Alison deigned to open her eyes.

But instead of acting completely mortified, Stephanie put her hands on her hips. "At least I *can* improve," she said. "What are you going to do?"

Patricia glared at Stephanie but she didn't answer.

Like Blaine, Patricia was blonde and blue-eyed, too. But she looked like a bleached-out copy. Her skin was milky pale. Her eyes were an expressionless china blue. And her thick, heavy, straight hair, cut in a chin-length chop that accentuated her square jaw, was so blonde it was almost white.

"Good. We're all here," said Clara, ignoring the whole exchange. She made a note in her book. "This is the order in which you will proceed down the aisle: Alison, Patricia, Kelly, Jamie, and Stephanie, since you're the maid of honor, you go last. The ushers will be waiting at the altar with the groom. The best man, as you know, is Mr. Alden's father."

"Gag me," muttered Stephanie.

Clara gave Stephanie a brief, stern look over the tops of her glasses and Stephanie shut up.

"You line up in order on the bride's side of the altar, the maid of honor closest to the bride. After the ceremony, the bride and groom exit first. Then the best man steps forward and ushers the maid of honor out, then the next usher steps forward and escorts the next bridesmaid out, and so on. Is that clear?"

"Big whoop," said Stephanie. "The ushers are a bunch of boring suits from Pres's office. Other girls have brothers who . . ."

They were never to find out what other girls had in brothers. Clara overrode Stephanie ruthlessly. "Does everybody have a rose? Good. These are to take the place of the bouquets that you will be carrying on Sunday. You hold the bouquets like this, at just below waist height.

"As soon as Ms. Harrod gets here, we'll begin. And that's all there is to it. Any questions?"

Patricia sniffed. "Nothing like walking the runways, is it?" she said to no one in particular. The way she said it made walking the runways sound low rent, even immoral somehow.

Alison raised one eyebrow. "Don't worry," she told Patricia in a bored voice. "I'm sure you'll catch on."

Jamie couldn't stop herself. She laughed aloud. Alison was funny — when her wit wasn't aimed at you.

"You're out of your league, Patty," said Stephanie.

"Don't call me Patty!" Patricia snapped. She let her china-blue eyes sweep over the bridesmaids. They dwelt malevolently, for a moment, on Jamie.

Then she looked away.

Stephanie giggled, her eyes bright with excitement. She was clearly a girl who thrived on excitement — of any kind. *Blaine would definitely get along with her new sister-in-law,* thought Jamie.

She looked at Patricia's rigid back. *But she definitely would never get along with Patricia, whatever their relationship became by marriage.*

Why was Patricia even in the wedding? Because she was related to Pres? If she'd been in love with him, it must hurt her.

She must hate Blaine, too. But then, Patricia so far had acted like she hated everybody. She made Alison, the ice queen, look warm and fuzzy.

Jamie almost felt sorry for Patricia. Almost. The music began.

Here comes the bride. Here comes the bride.

"Aren't we forgetting the bride?" asked Jamie. "Where's Blaine?"

Everyone stopped. Then Clara said, "I'm sorry. I should have mentioned it for those of you who didn't know. Traditionally, the bride doesn't participate in the rehearsal. She can watch, of course. I will be standing in for Blaine while she . . ."

"Oh, no you don't!" Blaine appeared, moving almost as fast as Stephanie had been. Her eyes were sparkling. "This is *my* show, and I'm going to be the star, even in the dress rehearsal!"

"I'd hardly call a wedding a show," remarked Patricia acidly.

"I'm glad to see you, too, Patricia," murmured Blaine. She took the rose from Clara's hand. "Now, Clara, don't argue. You knew this is what I've wanted to do all along. I think some of these traditions are just silly superstitions."

Clara said, in an expressionless voice, "If you insist."

"I do. Let's get this show on the road." Blaine smiled sweetly at Patricia.

The music grew and segued into the familiar wedding march.

Clara nodded. "Alison," she said.

Alison lifted her chin and glided forward, taking short steps, holding the rose in front of her as if it were a bouquet.

Even though it was only a rehearsal, Jamie felt her pulse quicken when it was her turn to walk forward. The ballroom was only half-decorated. The musicians playing the traditional tune were dressed not in formal black and white but in black turtlenecks and sweaters and jeans. Nevetheless, Jamie found herself caught by the magic.

No wonder brides felt like princesses in fairy tales, thought Jamie. She wondered if Blaine felt the same way.

But then, Blaine's whole life had been like a fairy tale, at least since she'd left Point Harbor.

Here comes the bride. Jamie looked up. Pres was standing at the altar, his hands in his pockets, his eyes on the bridesmaids.

It wasn't true that nobody noticed the bridesmaids, as Stephanie had complained. Pres clearly did. He watched Kelly with appreciative eyes as she walked sedately by. She flashed him a quick, dimpled smile and then took her place to one side of the altar.

He met Jamie's eyes. For one moment, she faltered in her walk, her cheeks burning.

He definitely made her come unwrapped.

Stop that, she scolded herself. *You pervert . . .*

The next pair of eyes she encountered almost stopped her in her tracks. Patricia was watching her intently. The naked hatred in her eyes made Jamie want to back up instead of walk forward.

Instead, she forced herself to keep walking. To shut everything out. She reached her place next to Kelly with a sigh of relief.

Stephanie practically pranced down the aisle, doing everything but throwing kisses.

Alison snorted derisively, but Jamie couldn't help but grin.

When it was Blaine's turn, Pres had eyes only for her. It was as if Jamie had imagined the whole thing.

Except that, unlike the ghost, Jamie knew she hadn't.

But the smiles that Blaine and Pres exchanged, so intimate, so warm, seemed real enough. Did Blaine really love Pres? Did Pres love Blaine?

Or was it just about money and power and chemistry. . . ?

Blaine moved in such a different world now. Was it a world where love and loyalty could survive?

The minister cleared his throat. "Dearly beloved," he began.

They stopped. They started. Clara darted in and out, making notes, delivering instructions about the ceremony. Pres pretended he had lost the ring. Even Pres's father, an older, unsmiling, much more reserved version of Pres, unbent enough to join in the rehearsal activity.

They practiced walking in and out again.

At last Clara decreed one final run-through.

"It's about time!" Stephanie cried. "My feet *hurt*. You're killing me! You're killing us all!" She ignored, with admirable calm, the crushing looks sent her way by her father, her brother.

Blaine said, "You hear that, Clara? How would you like for that to turn up in the newspapers? 'She killed the bride — and the wedding!' "

Pres's father transferred his disapproving look to Blaine.

Pres, unexpectedly, flushed. Then his face went blank.

Stephanie, predictably, giggled.

Clara only said, primly, "One more time. All the way through from the beginning."

* * *

The minister's voice became benevolent. Jamie brought her wandering thoughts back with a jerk from speculations of where Drew was and what he might be doing to the present. *Good. They were almost finished.*

She was definitely ready to party.

She hoped Drew was.

The minister paused. He looked around, beaming. He said, jovially, "Now, if anyone should have any reason why this man and this woman should not be joined in marriage . . ."

Something made Jamie look up.

The silk canopy that floated gently above them began to move. To belly out and bulge as if it had a life of its own.

Then, as Jamie watched with horrified eyes, it began to part down the center. It ripped with a thin, faintly protesting sound.

"Let them speak now . . ." the minister's voice trailed off.

He looked up.

They all looked up as the silk split open end to end.

And the doves came pouring out.

Only they didn't fly and coo.

They rained down in a lifeless, grotesque shower onto the bride.

Chapter 6

"Nooo!" Jamie gasped.

She lunged forward, half trying to save herself, half trying to reach her cousin.

She flinched back as the first horribly soft, horribly lifeless body glanced off her cheek.

And still they fell.

Blaine struck out wildly, sending the dead doves spinning out into the air in a grotesque parody of flight. People began to duck and scream.

"Get them off, get them off, get them off!" shouted Blaine.

Jamie stepped on something soft and felt it give with a sickening squish beneath her shoe.

Then Pres was grabbing Blaine's arm. "Blaine!" he shouted. "It's okay. It's just birds! They won't hurt you!"

Blaine swung around, mad with fear. Pres caught her other arm and forced her to stand still. She struggled for a moment longer, then suddenly went limp.

And as abruptly and awfully as it had begun, the rain of dead birds stopped.

Jamie heard Alison's cool voice say, "Kelly, let go. You're breaking my arm."

"Wow," breathed Stephanie. "Dead doves. I guess it *is* bad luck for the bride to be in the rehearsal!"

Jamie heard a strange sound. She turned in astonishment.

Patricia had begun to laugh.

By this time Clara had hurried forward. Pres turned on her. "Those birds were for the wedding, not the rehearsal! What the hell is going on here!" he barked.

Clara said, in her most colorless voice, "I don't know."

Looking down at the birds lying lifeless and cold at his feet, Pres kicked several to one side. "We've rehearsed enough," he said. "We're going."

"Perhaps if Blaine could lie down and rest," suggested Clara.

But Blaine, who had been leaning against Pres, lifted her head. Her face was unnaturally pale, her eyes almost unnaturally bright.

"No, I'm fine," she insisted. "It was probably just . . . just an accident."

"I've sent for the bird handler," Clara said.

Blaine managed a small smile. "Efficient Clara. . . . I just need a few minutes to pull myself together. Then . . . why don't we just go party and forget all this?"

"Are you sure?" asked Pres, taking Blaine's face between his hands and looking down into it. "You don't have to, you know."

"Yes, I'm sure," said Blaine. Her eyes met Pres's solemnly. "Very, very sure," she added, so softly that Jamie was sure it was meant for Pres's ears only.

The grim expression left Pres's face. Blaine smiled and he smiled back and leaned forward to wrap his arms around her and kiss her lightly on the lips.

Blaine said, "I'm not about to let a dead dove spoil my wedding . . . ow . . . Pres, you're gonna squeeze the life out of me, if you're not careful."

"Sorry." Pres released her abruptly and stepped back. He raised his voice. "Well, what are we all waiting for here — let's go to a party."

Hastily the wedding party began to pick its way among the fallen birds, the pale, softly feathered bodies, the dark staring eyes. Jamie shuddered and wished she could look away. But she couldn't. Even after she'd gotten free of the spill of doves and was almost to the door, she kept looking down, expecting to see one.

To feel it squishing horribly beneath her feet.

Kelly and Alison were ahead of her. Stephanie came up to walk beside Jamie.

"Gross, huh?" she said enthusiastically.

"Totally," agreed Jamie, making her tone unencouraging.

But Stephanie Alden was impervious to snubs. "Boy, Pres is like, completely maximally furious! Did you see his face?"

Jamie shook her head.

With a giggle, Stephanie said, "I bet Pats *loved* it, what do you bet?"

They passed Clara, who was speaking sternly to a slight, intense-looking young man whose long hair was pulled back into a ponytail.

"An explanation . . ." they heard her say.

"Hey, they're my birds. I'm the one who should be upset!" he protested. "I don't know how they got there, okay?" His voice trailed off as Alison and Kelly walked by.

Alison stared at him haughtily, her lip curling.

Then Clara said, "Excuse me. That's not the point, is it?"

Stephanie said, "He's gonna wish he was

one of those birds, by the time Clara is finished with him. Not that I think it was an accident, do you?"

"What are you talking about?" Jamie asked.

Stephanie looked surprised. And then uncertain. "I mean, it couldn't have been an accident, could it? Someone had to kill them before they put them up there, didn't they? Otherwise, we would have heard them while we rehearsed. Someone had to have done that on purpose. To get back at Blaine. To ruin her wedding rehearsal."

Jamie suddenly flashed on the image of the ghostly bride. But she pushed it away. "Are you saying Patricia . . ."

With a quick, almost violent shake of her head, Stephanie said, "No! I don't think even Patricia would do something like that."

But her voice lacked conviction.

Jamie stopped. She turned and looked back at the shambles before the altar. The hotel crew had already gotten up most of the dead birds. The handler was kneeling down, gathering them, tenderly and sadly, into a bag. Someone had come in with a ladder and was setting it up beneath the torn silk.

Clara, holding her ubiquitous notebook, was standing above the handler, still talking sternly.

Patricia was nowhere in sight. Where had she gone to so quickly?

Patricia had laughed when the doves came tumbling down, Jamie remembered. She hadn't even acted surprised.

"Smothered," repeated Kelly with relish. "The handler said they'd all been smothered. He said they'd been dead a long time. They're trying to find out who put them in the cage up there ahead of time. He never puts them in until right before the ceremony, he says, because so many things can go wrong."

"Could we stop talking about this, please?" said Alison, snagging a glass of champagne off the tray of a passing waiter.

"Great party," said Jamie, obediently trying to change the subject. And to conceal the fact that she was looking for Drew.

Alison suddenly snickered. "That's pathetic, Jamie. But it was nice of you to try."

"Why don't you like the party?" asked a smooth, chilly voice. "Too rich for your blood?"

"Patricia," said Jamie. "Where did *you* go?"

Patricia, almost but not quite, looked down her nose at Jamie. "Go? What are you talking about?"

"When all the birds, you know, fell? Suddenly you just weren't there!"

"Well, excuse me," said Patricia. "I didn't know that being a member of the wedding required me to stand around ankle deep in dead birds. . . . I went to change, obviously."

It was true. *Patricia has changed her clothes, if not her attitude,* thought Jamie.

Flushing slightly, Jamie shrugged. Somehow, she didn't really mind it so much when Alison was witchy. But Jamie would have liked nothing better than to punch Patricia in her snobby nose.

Then she saw Drew and forgot all about Patricia.

He was dodging in and out among the clumps of people toward them, holding two drinks in his hand.

"Here," he said, thrusting one toward her as he came up to join them.

Jamie took it cautiously. She hadn't liked the champagne she'd tasted at other weddings. She didn't think her tastes had changed.

But this wasn't champagne . . . was it? "What is it?" she said.

"The drink of models everywhere. Right, Kelly?" Drew said, giving his older sister a sly look. "Seltzer and lemon."

"Oh. Thanks!" Jamie said with much more enthusiasm.

She saw Alison's slight smile and made a face back. Alison's smile grew infinitesimally.

"I hear you had some big excitement," said Drew softly to Jamie.

Wrinkling her nose, Jamie said, "Yuk. Don't tell me you missed it."

Drew said, "Okay, I won't . . . but it doesn't sound as if it was an accident, either."

Jamie took a sip of drink. "Maybe it was just a stupid joke."

"A stupid, cruel joke, sounds like to me," said Drew, sipping his own drink and letting his gaze roam the room. "Everyone seems to be cool about it, though."

"You think so?" said Patricia, wedging herself so suddenly into the conversation that Jamie almost jumped. "I don't think so. I think that all everyone is talking about right now is those dead birds. They're not talking about the wedding. They're not talking about the beautiful bride. They're talking dead birds."

She leaned slightly forward and her face contorted. "Blaine doesn't love Pres, you know. She saw a rich man and she went after him. She's marrying him for his money. For an easy life."

"That's not true!" said Jamie, any pity she

had ever felt for Patricia evaporating in the heat of anger. "Blaine has a career, she has plenty of money of her own."

"Does she?" Patricia smiled. "Her career will only last as long as her face."

Alison murmured, "At least she had a career."

Patricia went on viciously, "When her face goes, she'll just be another anorectic has-been, living on savings and a bunch of old photographs. If she doesn't marry Pres, she's nobody. Nobody, do you hear me? And she could still end up that way!"

Turning on her heel, Patricia stalked away.

"Don't hold anything back," said Alison sardonically.

"It's not true!" Jamie cried. "Blaine isn't marrying Pres for his money."

Kelly shrugged. "What if she is? Pres is a great-looking guy. It's a good deal, Jamie. Alison used to think so, didn't you, Alison darling?"

"Shut up, Kelly darling," said Alison.

Drew cut in. "Hey, what's the dif? Come on, Jamie, let's go check this party out." To Alison and Kelly he said, "See you guys later."

"Amazing party," he said lightly, grabbing Jamie's hand and leading her away. "So . . . do you like to watch?"

"I don't know," said Jamie. She looked up at him from beneath her eyelashes. "I know you do . . ."

Drew grinned wickedly. "I do. And I know the perfect place. Follow me." Still holding her hand, he began to head across the room.

"Where are we going?" asked Jamie.

"You'll see. You've just got to trust me. Gotta believe."

They left the ballroom and Drew led her down a maze of corridors, pushing open one door and then another. Each door seemed to lead to a narrower, dingier corridor. More than one door said, "Do Not Enter" and "Staff Only."

But Drew ignored the warnings. At last he pushed open a door and stepped back triumphantly. "Check it out."

A staircase wound upward into the dark.

For a moment, Jamie hesitated. She felt Drew's fingers tighten around her own. They were warm. She was intensely aware of the feel of his skin against hers.

What are you afraid of? she thought. *What do you think is going to happen?*

I don't know, she answered herself.

And smiled in the dark. *Anything.*

Everything.

Drew went through the door and tugged on

her hand. His face looked back down at hers from the shadows. One corner of his mouth lifted in a slight smile.

She followed him, let him lead her up and up in the dizzying darkness.

At last he stopped again. He pushed open another door and they stepped into the narrowest corridor of all. The wall on one side of the corridor had several doors in it. The wall on the other side had neither windows nor doors. It was blank. The only light came from dim light directly above the door.

"Where are we?" she asked, lowering her voice instinctively.

In answer, Drew led her to the first door in the corridor and pushed it open. He stepped to one side and motioned her forward. Stooping slightly, for the door was small and low, Jamie went in.

She was standing in a shallow, unlit alcove. Then Drew reached out. She saw that he had caught hold of the edge of a curtain. He pulled it slightly to one side.

The shallow, hidden alcove was a secret window that looked down onto the ballroom. The whole glittering party was spread out far, far below.

"All the ballrooms have these sorts of box seats. . . . The curtains make them look like windows, but they're not. The real windows are on the other two walls."

"This is totally great," said Jamie, parting the curtain slightly and leaning forward to stare at the swirl of people below.

"I know," said Drew, his voice so profoundly self-satisfied that it drew a ripple of laughter from Jamie.

He smiled good-naturedly and leaned against her. His arms slipped around her.

"You know what I think? I think people used these to meet their forbidden lovers at the parties. You can see without being seen, if you stay in the shadow of the curtain."

Jamie shivered. She shivered at the touch of Drew's arms. But she also shivered at the sudden, unbidden memory of the ghostly Rose.

Had Rose met her lover here? Had he stolen up there to peer down and watch her dance in all her finery? To wait until she could slip away for whispered words and forbidden kisses behind these very curtains? In this very box?

For a moment, a faint chill touched her flesh. *Get a life,* she told herself. *Grow up. There's no such thing as ghosts.*

Besides, those definitely weren't ghostly fingers touching her neck now. The hand that was sending shivers down her spine was warm and very human.

She turned her head slightly to look at Drew. Then she stepped back and lifted her face to his in the delicious darkness.

Below, the wedding guests partied on. People laughed and talked, flirted and pouted. They struck poses and made plans. And Blaine was the center of it all, the beautiful blushing bride. No one who saw her laugh and smile, who watched her look up at her handsome fiancé from beneath her sinfully long eyelashes, would ever think she was anything but the star of a perfect wedding.

In the curtained darkness above the party glitter, Jamie forgot about the wedding. She forgot about her famous, beautiful cousin. She forgot about her mother's warning.

She forgot everything.

Until the lights went out.

Even then, Jamie didn't realize that something was wrong. The little shrieks of half-frightened laughter, the babble of rising voices, only penetrated her consciousness gradually.

When it did, she pulled away from Drew just enough to murmur "Drew?"

"Mmm," said Drew, pulling her closer again.

"Everyone stay calm," a voice ordered from below.

"Drew, something's wrong."

"Keep your eyes closed," he murmured. "You'll never notice."

Another voice, loud and reassuring, said, "Nothing to worry about. Stay where you are and the lights will be back on in a minute."

Jamie half-turned her head and looked down from their hiding place. The tiny flares of matches and lighters had begun to prick the darkness. *It was sort of pretty*, Jamie thought hazily. *Like being at a concert.*

Drew said, "You heard the man. He said don't move." His arms tightened around her again. Jamie leaned against him. She felt his warm breath against her hair.

But suddenly he jerked back.

"Drew?" she said.

"Oh, my god," he said hoarsely. "It can't be."

"Can't be what?" she asked.

"Don't you smell it?"

"Smell what?"

"Smoke. It's a fire!"

Chapter 7

"FIRE!" a voice below suddenly cried.

"No," said Jamie. But even as she spoke, she knew it was true. This was not the smoke that came with dreams of ghostly brides. It was real, the smoke of nightmares. It burned her eyes and filled her nose, and each second it seemed to thicken in the darkness.

"We've got to get out of here!" said Drew. Grabbing Jamie's hand, he turned toward the back of the box and pushed blindly outward at the door.

It seemed even darker in the corridor. Or was it the smoke, growing thicker, more malignant.

"STAY WHERE YOU ARE!" someone bellowed above the screams rising from the black pit behind them.

"Drew, *wait*." Jamie caught his arm and pulled him back. "Shut the door."

"We can't stay here," said Drew.

"If we get lost trying to find our way out, we could get trapped. Here we have a chance!"

"No one knows where we are," said Drew. But he shut the door and stepped back to the edge of the balcony.

At least we won't be trampled to death, thought Jamie grimly, listening to the cries that pierced the seething darkness beneath the balcony's edge. Her hand tightened on Drew's. Where was Blaine? Kelly? Alison? Would they know enough not to get caught in the panic? To stay out of the way?

Jamie realized she was trembling. She pressed back against Drew and felt his arms go around her. It comforted her. A little.

Then Jamie saw it.

A shimmering figure high above the crowd, hovering there like a flaming angel.

An avenging angel, thought Jamie irrelevantly.

"Drew," she managed to say. "Do you see her?"

"Yes," answered Drew softly.

It was the bride. The ghostly bride.

Someone else looked and saw the apparition. Someone else screamed what Jamie had only thought.

"It's her! She's come back for revenge.

She's going to kill us all! It's the bride!"

Then, suddenly, the lights came on.

Jamie blinked in the blinding brightness.

And the bride was gone.

Jamie blinked again. The air, which she had expected to be thick and white with smoke, was not.

The doors of the small ballroom burst open. The firefighters had arrived.

"A stupid false alarm," said Kelly indignantly. She yanked her shirt over her head and dropped it on the floor. Her voice echoed hollowly behind her as she disappeared into the bathroom. "They couldn't even find out what caused the smoke smell."

She emerged a moment later swathed in an elaborate bathrobe, looking like a glamour queen from the old movies Jamie's mother and father liked to vid out on. "Well, if you ask me, Jamie . . ."

"Did you ask her, Jamie?" asked Alison's lazy voice. Alison glided through the door that connected her room to Kelly's. To Jamie's surprise, she realized that Alison was wearing plaid flannel pj's and fuzzy scuffs.

"Even if you didn't ask her," Alison went on, curling up on a chair, "she'll tell you. Won't you, Kell?"

Kelly sniffed. "All I'm saying is that that ghost wasn't a false alarm."

"Did everyone see the ghost?"

"No. But everyone believes they did now," said Alison cynically. "Same dif."

Kelly said indignantly, "And you know what the hotel manager and the firefighters are saying? They're saying it was mass hysteria. Huh."

"It could have been some kind of a prank," said Jamie. "Like what happened with the doves."

"The smoke, maybe. But not the ghost. They searched all over and they couldn't find anything," Kelly argued. "That proves it was a ghost, doesn't it? I mean, how else could it have gotten up there, hovered around, and then just disappeared without a trace?"

"That doesn't prove it was a ghost, Kelly, it just proves that they didn't find anything," said Alison. "They said there was a whole maze of corridors and doors and things behind those walls, remember?"

Jamie looked up. "Maybe it *was* a ghost," she said. "Maybe the smoke was part of it."

Alison and Kelly stared at Jamie. Then Kelly said, "That's it! You're a genius."

"Ghost smoke," murmured Alison. "Interesting."

"It's a haunted wedding," Kelly went on excitedly. "Don't you see? That's what killed the doves! That's what caused the smell of smoke with *no fire*. It's the ghost. The ghost bride. She's come back to haunt Blaine's wedding!"

Jamie opened the door and slid silently out of her room. It was very late. Very empty. Very quiet.

Early really. The darkest hour of the night, the one just before the dawn.

Returning from Kelly and Alison's room, Jamie had slipped carefully out of her borrowed clothes and hastily into her luxurious bed. But she had not slipped easily into sleep.

After a while she gave up and called the front desk.

They'd been surprised by her request. But no doubt they'd had stranger requests and at odder hours. Shortly after they'd assured her the matter would be promptly taken care of, two members of the hotel staff had come and taken the mirror away.

Now the corner was empty. But Jamie hadn't been able to empty her mind of the memories of the evening's events.

Of the hauntings.

I don't believe in ghosts, Jamie told herself. But if she didn't, what had happened had to have a human explanation. And the human behind it would have to be, in his or her own way, even more unpleasant than a ghost. Unpleasant — and diabolically clever and cruel.

Someone who was willing to kill dozens of doves and arrange for them to pour down upon a wedding rehearsal in gruesome warning. To turn off lights and fill the air with the smell of smoke and to make a ghostly bride hover above a darkened ballroom.

What if the guests hadn't stayed calm? What if they'd panicked? In the mad dash for the door, people surely would have been trampled and crushed.

Killed, even.

Sleep wouldn't come. Jamie tossed and turned. She got up and tried to read. She climbed back into the tangled sheets and blankets and closed her eyes again.

And saw Blaine's pale, set face as the dead birds rained down around her, saw Blaine looking up at Pres in fear and bewilderment.

Who would want to hurt Blaine like this? And why?

Almost immediately, Jamie flashed on haughty, scornful Patricia. Patricia hated Blaine, no question. But did she hate her enough to rig those stunts? Would Patricia be able to do something like that?

Where had Patricia been when the lights went out?

By the time Drew and Jamie had made their way back through the maze of corridors to join the other guests, who'd been evacuated from that end of the building, there was no way of telling. People had scattered, some to the restaurant or to the bar, others to the smaller rooms around the hotel, others to pursuits of their own.

Blaine had been standing in the lobby, the color rushing and ebbing from her cheeks, her eyes unnaturally bright.

"Just a series of nasty old accidents," she kept saying, over and over. "Isn't that right, Pres, darling? It could have happened to anyone. It's nobody's fault, is it, Pres?"

Pres, pale and silent beside her, his jaw clenched, had merely nodded.

How he must have hated the commotion! He'd defied his parents to marry Blaine and now this. Worse still if it got into the newspapers . . .

Was it possible that Stephanie and Patricia weren't the enemies they seemed to be? That they were working together, Stephanie to prevent the wedding and save the family honor, Patricia because Pres had done her wrong?

Nah. You've been watching too many weird

movies, Jamie told herself. But she sat up anyway, frowning in thought.

There was Alison, of course. What was it that Kelly had said about Alison and Pres? That Alison had once thought marriage to Pres would be a pretty good package?

Had Alison been in love with Pres once? Had he dumped her for Blaine? He'd clearly dated lots of girls, if what Stephanie had said was true.

Before Blaine, Alison had been the flavor of the month, the hottest model in town. Had she been Pres's girlfriend, too, before Blaine?

The enmity between Alison and Blaine was no secret. Even though they'd started out in the business at the same time, even though they had once shared an apartment, everyone knew that Alison and Blaine, dangerous enough on their own, were completely out of control around each other.

Even Jamie had heard the story of how Blaine had accidentally — or not — stabbed Alison's hand with the letter opener.

It never would have happened if it had been anyone else but Alison, Jamie was sure of that.

But then, some people had said the whole thing was staged for publicity. That Alison and Blaine had planned it. That both of them were known to love the spotlight, the limelight, and were unscrupulous in their pursuit of publicity.

Publicity.

A sudden, unpleasant thought occurred to Jamie.

Was the publicity of marrying Pres not enough? Was it even remotely possible that Blaine was behind everything, that Blaine was staging the whole haunted wedding for publicity?

"No! Not possible," Jamie said aloud, pushing the unwelcome speculation away.

Even as she pushed her feet out of the bed.

She dressed quickly in her black jeans and black turtleneck. A moment later she was walking out her door.

The heavy carpets swallowed every sound. She passed no one on the stairs. The elevator hung motionless in its shaft. The vast lobby was empty.

She stopped at the bottom of the stairs and pulled back. She was almost certain that the night manager wouldn't let her go where she wanted to go. Or at best, would insist on going with her.

No to both choices, she thought. She looked quickly around and spotted the phone on the far wall. If she could make it to the booth without being seen . . .

The night manager turned a page of the book he was reading. He yawned.

Jamie dove across the space to the phone booth.

Silence.

Without giving herself time to think, Jamie dialed the phone. When the night manager answered she said, "I think someone is stuck in the elevator. It sounded like someone shouting. Could you check it out immediately, please? I'd like to get some sleep." She slammed down the phone, hoping she would sound like an irate guest. And that the night manager wouldn't hear the phone being hung up and realize where it was coming from.

She waited. She heard the creak of hinges as the low door to the desk swung open. Leaning out from her hiding place, she saw the manager cross the lobby toward the elevators.

His back was to hers. Now or never.

Jamie sped across the lobby, which had carpeting as blissfully thick and soundproof as the carpets in the halls. A moment later she was racing down the corridor toward the small ballroom.

The doors were shut. She pushed them, half-expecting them to be locked. But they weren't. She stuck her head in cautiously and looked around. Not even a faint smell of smoke lingered in the air. The room was dark and empty, filled only with a vast, whispery silence.

Leaving the ballroom door ajar so she would have light from the hallway, Jamie slipped inside. She didn't know what she expected to find. If it was a clue, she was too late. The cleaning crew had already been through. The room was neat and sterile and ready for the next party.

Jamie went to the middle of the room and looked up at the curtain behind which she and Drew had been standing when the lights went out. The ghost had appeared from behind the curtains in the box across the ballroom.

Ghost, thought Jamie, *or someone dressed up to look like a ghost*. Grimly, she pushed aside the memory of the ghostly bride reaching out from the mirror in her room. *That had been a dream*, she told herself. *Only a dream*.

Crossing the ballroom, Jamie made her way from one door to another, looking for a way into the maze of passages that would lead to the box where the ghost had appeared. At last she found one that opened onto a spiral staircase identical to the one that she and Drew had climbed.

The stairway was dark. She groped her way along the wall, found a light switch. A dim light pierced the gloom. Barely.

Jamie wished she had a flashlight. But it was too late to think about that now. Taking a deep breath, she went up the stairs.

The hall at the top of the stairs was dark, too. She turned that light on and then found another hall and another light and then another until at last she came to the narrow passage lined with doors. This time, the doors were on the left and the blank wall was on the right.

The light there was no brighter than anywhere else.

She was suddenly aware of how alone she was. How easily she could be lost and not found, perhaps for days.

Perhaps not ever.

Stop that, she told herself. Taking another deep breath, she walked toward the first door. The door that opened onto where the ghost had been standing.

She reached out to grasp the handle and stopped.

Frowned.

Had she heard something? She looked quickly back over her shoulder. But the dim, dusty corridor was empty, and the door at the end through which she'd entered was closed.

Nothing, she thought. *It was nothing. Nerves. Imagination.*

You're imagining a ghost on the other side of that door. A ghost that isn't real. That doesn't exist.

Her fingers touched the handle.

She jerked back.

The handle had moved beneath her hand.

The door began to swing open.

Chapter 8

She screamed, or thought she screamed. She hurled herself with all her might at the door to slam it shut, to keep whatever was on the other side from getting out.

The door almost closed.

She almost won.

Then slowly, in spite of everything she could do, it began to swing open.

She was panting, sobbing. Trying to force it shut. Fighting desperately, vainly.

Then she heard it: A voice saying her name.

But it wasn't a ghostly voice. It was a familiar one.

For a moment longer she lay pressed against the door with all her might.

Then she whispered, "Drew?" and her legs gave way and she slid to the floor.

Drew wedged himself out of the partially opened door.

"Jamie! Jamie, what are you doing here?"

"What are *you* doing here?" she shot back, angry at how frightened she'd been, angry that he'd seen her so vulnerable.

Drew sat down beside her and put his hand on her arm. "It's okay," he said. "I'm sorry if I scared you."

"You didn't," she said, narrowing her eyes and lifting her chin and daring him to call her a liar.

He didn't take the dare. Instead he said, "Well, you scared me. I must have fallen asleep. Some ghostbuster I am, huh?"

"Is *that* what you were doing?" asked Jamie. She was glad to feel her heart slowing down, her breathing returning to normal. She began to forgive Drew. A little.

She allowed herself to lean against him. His arm slid easily behind her shoulders.

"That's what I was doing, too," she confessed. "Have you been up here all night?"

"Yep. I waited till all the suits and uniforms cleared out, then I came back, uh, unobserved. Did a Sherlock Holmes, but I didn't find anything."

"What, no clues?" she asked mockingly.

"None. Nada. Whoever it was, they were good. And fast."

"Or supernatural," Jamie couldn't help but

add. Maybe she was hoping that Drew would laugh. Or do an Alison and tell her she had a vivid imagination.

He didn't. His arm tightened momentarily around her shoulders and then he said, conversationally, "You know, the hotel management, or at least the clerk I talked to, denied any knowledge of a ghost bride. Said he'd never even heard the rumor."

"Yeah, *right*," said Jamie. "They have to say that. Ghosts are bad for business. Especially weddings."

"True," Drew answered. He paused. "So what now?"

Jamie looked at her watch. "It's dawn," she said, with some surprise. "This is the first time I've ever spent the night with a ghost."

"Or a guy?" suggested Drew teasingly.

"I'm hungry," Jamie said quickly. "Aren't you? Want to go get some breakfast?"

"So many appetites, so little time," Drew said sadly.

Jamie jumped up. She reached down and pulled Drew to his feet. "Breakfast," she said firmly. "I'm talking about breakfast."

Drew leaned closer. "You know what they say," he said. "Life is uncertain. Eat dessert first."

* * *

"There's a pancake left," Drew pointed out. "You must have overlooked it."

"Thanks," said Jamie. She made the pancake platter-to-plate transfer, then drowned the pancake in maple syrup, and forked up a bite.

"Ook," she said, waving her fork. "Aine."

"Why yes, I do believe it is Blaine," said Drew. "Aine! Over here!"

Blaine turned, a puzzled look on her face. The expression changed to one of pleased surprise as she made her way across the deserted dining area toward Jamie and Drew. To Jamie's amazement, she saw that Blaine was wearing gray sweatpants and an old red sweatshirt over a white turtleneck sweater. Her hair was carelessly pulled back with a scrunchie. But she still looked completely together and completely at ease.

Jamie held up the pancake-laden fork and waved it.

"That should get the waiter's attention," Drew teased.

"Darlings," Blaine said, sitting down. "I slept like the dead. Did you? Sleep okay, I mean?"

"We did," said Drew.

Blaine raised her eyebrows, looking from Jamie to Drew to Jamie again. "I'm glad to hear it. But you shock me."

Color flooded Jamie's face.

Drew grinned.

Blaine went on, "I thought I'd be the first one up, but you two beat me." She yawned and stretched her arms over her head. "Sorry."

A waiter appeared.

"Gallons of coffee," Blaine ordered, "and whatever she's having."

She drank her first cup of coffee in silence, staring out of the windows across the terrace to the empty shore lashed by the waves. The sun had only just come up, bringing with it the promise of a cold, beautiful day.

"I'm glad I got to see you," said Blaine. "Are you having fun, Jamie? At the rehearsal, I mean."

"Yes," said Jamie.

"It's been very interesting," said Drew.

"Hasn't it?" said a cool voice. "A diet Coke and black coffee," it continued, and then Patricia slid into the seat next to Drew as the waiter hurried away. She dropped a folded newspaper she was holding onto the table.

"That's what the newspapers think, too. Only interesting isn't the word they're using."

"HOT, HAUNTED WEDDING," the headline read.

Blaine frowned. "What?"

"My, we do eat a lot, don't we?" Patricia said, as the pancakes arrived.

Jamie stared at Patricia. She was wearing a skin-tight silver unitard, over which she'd pulled a pair of navy compression shorts with silver stripes down the sides. Over it all she was wearing a silver and navy supplex jacket. "But then you might be able to work some of it off. The hotel has a very well-equipped gym."

"Oh? Did you meet someone there?" asked Jamie, keeping her face innocent.

Blaine said, suddenly and explosively, "I don't believe this! *How* are they getting this information? How?"

"You're just a publicity magnet," said Patricia. "But that's what you wanted. Isn't it? Too bad it isn't what Pres wants."

Blaine's fingers crumpled the newspaper into a wad. But she smiled at Patricia sweetly. "Clearly I'm a better judge of what Pres wants than you are, Patricia. Now, if you'll excuse me."

She stood up. To Jamie she said, "I might try to get Alison and Kelly to join me in the gym later, if you want to come. They can give you any gear you might need."

"Cool," said Jamie. "I'm definitely going to check it out."

She crammed the last bite of pancake in her mouth and said, for Patricia's benefit, "These were great! If you've already been to the gym, Patricia, I bet you can have pancakes. Just this once. . . . See ya."

"Ah, me, too," Drew said hastily, following suit.

"Wonderful how Patricia brings out the worst in people, isn't it," said Blaine softly as they left Pres's ex glaring after them from the table.

They stopped at the entrance to the restaurant to sign the charges for breakfast to their rooms. As Blaine scribbled her name across the bottom of her bill, she looked up at the waiter thoughtfully from under her long, dark lashes. Suddenly the corners of her eyes crinkled with glee. She handed the check back to the waiter and nodded in Patricia's direction. "Would you please take my friend over there the complete pancake breakfast, with bacon, and add whipped cream on the pancakes? Bill it to me . . ."

The bodies were pumping. Sweating. Hips thrusting and legs tightening and relaxing.

And all the time they watched themselves in silver mirrors, touching their tongues to their lips, tossing their heads. The ladies who lycraed. The boys who buffed.

I've never seen so many naked . . . egos, thought Jamie.

The Sandhill gym was sleek, but as spare as the rest of the hotel was posh. The equipment was so new that it was practically futuristic.

In her old sweats, with her hair pulled back with a sweatband, Jamie didn't match the image of the handful of pumped, high-gloss people working out. But they didn't notice. They were too busy watching themselves become perfect.

And more perfect.

Jamie did the weight drill she'd learned on the basketball team, keeping an eye out for someone she knew, hoping that Kelly and Alison and Blaine would show up. She'd knocked on their doors, but no one had been around.

Who knows what trouble they're out getting into, she thought. *Maybe they're ghost-hunting.*

She smiled, remembering her own pre-dawn ghost hunt.

As she did the drills, the weight room emptied out even more. Forgetting after a while about the lycra suits surrounding her, Jamie let herself go. Each machine made her stronger, made her remember that she was sturdy. Not easily shaken.

Not afraid.

Not afraid of a bogus ghost and some sick practical joker who was out to ruin a wedding.

By the time she was finished, she was sweating, too. And panting unfashionably loudly. A woman riding an exercise bike and reading a fashion mag gave Jamie an annoyed look.

Jamie gave her a big grin and the woman looked hastily back down at the magazine, flipping it with long, red fingernails that gave her occupation away: a woman of leisure, a woman who did nothing, a woman for whom everything was paid for — as long as she kept her looks.

Was it worth it, Jamie wondered. She didn't think so.

She turned away, still panting. Hot tub here I come, she thought. She looked for the attendant to find out what the rules were, but he was across the room, ostensibly showing another guest how she could get the most out of the stair-stepper.

Jamie shrugged and headed for the lockers. She changed to her bathing suit and, throwing her towel over her shoulder, went in search of the hot tub.

Not that she'd ever been in one. But she was pretty sure she would like it.

It was on a small, private terrace overlooking the ocean. Sliding open the glass door, she plunged through the cold air and into the deep, steaming water. Delicious. Decadent.

Definitely decent.

She was right. She liked it.

With a sigh, she leaned her head back against the redwood rim of the tub to watch the whitecaps curling on the distant waves. The continuing murmur of the ocean was punctuated by the faint shrieks of gulls. Other than that, she might have been alone in the world.

The water lapped gently against her skin. She closed her eyes and slid into a pleasant fantasy.

"Does it feel good?" a voice whispered softly in her ear.

Jamie jumped and water splashed noisily out of the tub.

"Hey, take it easy. It's just me." Pres slid down into the water to sit next to her. "I was going to the sauna, but I suddenly decided the hot tub looked nice." He paused and his eyes surveyed Jamie. "Very, very nice."

Jamie forced herself to meet his eyes through the curls of steam. "Yes," she said, refusing to be drawn in.

"So are you enjoying the wedding, cousin? We will be cousins, you know, after tomorrow."

"True," said Jamie, sliding deeper into the water, wishing, somehow, that her bathing suit was a body suit. And that his was, too.

"It's quite a wedding, isn't it. Not the usual thing. But then, Blaine's not your usual woman.

"I have to admit, it's taken my family a little while to get used to the idea. But they're going to love Blaine. And she's going to love them."

Relaxing slightly, Jamie said, "Blaine's terrific."

"Yes," said Pres. "I know."

A small silence fell. Jamie said brightly, "Well, I've been in here long enough. See ya!"

Feeling Pres's amused eyes on her, she hastily got out of the hot tub, wrapping the towel around her.

"See you — cousin," Pres said, his lazy voice following her as she hurried away.

Wow, you are so cool, Jamie told herself mockingly. *What do you think Pres is going to do to you, anyway? He's marrying your cousin Blaine tomorrow, Haroldson. Get a grip.*

But she couldn't hide the fact from herself that Pres felt dangerous — and dangerously attractive. And that it wasn't just the heat from the hot tub that was making her breathe so fast as she hurried away.

Annoyed that she had run from Pres, and from the pleasure of soaking in the hot tub, Jamie slowed down. Checked it out. Sauna, Pres had said. Yes. She'd do some time in the sauna.

That could be very nice, too. . . .

The sauna was as empty as the rest of the club. The rules posted seemed pretty simple. Don't turn the heat up too high. Don't stay in too long. Don't leave any newspapers or magazines in it because they might spontaneously combust in the dry heat.

Spontaneous combustion, thought Jamie. *Interesting.*

She pushed the door open and stepped inside. The heat hit her like a blow. It seemed to burn her nostrils and sizzle along her skin.

The sauna was small and dimly lit and, like the hot tub, made of wood, with wooden benches lining the walls. Jamie walked toward the corner, feeling herself break into a sweat as she did so. She spread out her towel and lay down.

Relax, she told herself. *You're having fun.*

She closed her eyes and drifted.

"Having fun?" said Pres's voice.

Jamie sat up, forcing herself not to grab for the towel. Pres sauntered into the sauna, his own towel around his waist.

"You're finished in the hot tub?" Jamie asked, hearing the squeak in her voice and despising it. *Duh, Jamie*, she thought in despair.

"Nice. But boring all alone," said Pres. "I didn't know you were going to be in the sauna. That makes it much nicer . . . that is, if you don't mind me joining you."

"N-no. Of course not."

To her relief, Pres sat down in the far corner. He yawned. "In some countries, you know, they sit in saunas until they're very, very hot. Then they run out and roll in the snow."

"That would wake you up," said Jamie inanely. She lay back down before she could say — or do — anything else majorly stupid and covered her eyes with one arm.

"Or kill you," said Pres with a soft laugh. The laugh made him sound more human, somehow. Maybe it was all an act, thought Jamie. Like so much in Blaine's world. Maybe when Blaine and Pres got together, they dropped the acts and were able to . . . to . . . spontaneously combust.

A wry smile twisted Jamie's mouth.

The room got hotter. Hotter.

And hotter.

And hotter still.

Jamie shifted slightly. Then she sat up. Sweat had pooled in the hollow of her throat. It trickled from beneath her arms and down her sides.

She was drenched in sweat.

"Whoa," she said. She looked over at Pres and said, deliberately, "This is too hot for me to handle."

She saw the flash of Pres's teeth as he smiled. But all he said was, "Yeah. Takes some getting used to."

Jamie stood up. She felt as if she were moving in slow motion. For a moment, the room spun crazily before her eyes.

"Are you all right?" Pres asked.

Jamie started to nod, then thought better of it. No point in making herself even dizzier. "Yep," she said. "Soon as I get into something cooler."

Pres laughed.

Pleased at having kept her composure at last around the rich and famous Pres Alden,

Jamie reached out and pushed the door of the sauna. It was a heavy door. It didn't give.

She gave it another push. Even that slight effort made her breathe harder, made her sweat.

"Here," said Pres. "Let me help." He got up and came to the door and pushed it.

He pushed again.

He frowned and stepped back. Then he threw the whole weight of his shoulder against the door.

It didn't budge.

"I don't believe this," he said.

"What is it?" said Jamie. Her breath was coming in gasps.

"The door. It's stuck. We're trapped!"

Chapter 9

I'm going to spontaneously combust, thought Jamie, hysteria rising inside.

No. No. Stay calm, she ordered herself.

"Are you sure? Let me help." To her surprise, her voice sounded unworried. Almost soothing.

She stepped up beside Pres and leaned her shoulder against the door.

"Ready?" asked Pres. "One, two, three, *push*."

But the door held. It didn't give an inch.

"Maybe we could find something to pry it open," Jamie said, panting. She turned, her gaze sweeping the small, dim room. She blinked. The walls seemed to pulsate in the heat. She ran her tongue over her lips. Although she was sweating furiously, her mouth was dry.

The room was bare. And hot.

So hot.

She turned back around. Pres ran his hands along the edges of the door, trying to find a crack, a place to wedge his fingers and attempt to pry it open. But the door was tightly sealed.

"We can't panic," said Pres. "We haven't been in here long enough for it to hurt us."

But his voice didn't sound as sure as his words. And he, too, was breathing heavily, while sweat ran in rivulets down his face, neck, and chest.

"We can call for help," said Jamie. "If we shout together, they'll hear us." But who would hear them? The guy in charge, so involved with the lady in lycra on the stairstepper? The others in the weight room, so involved with themselves? And all of them so far, far away?

She didn't say that. She saved her breath for the shouting.

The screaming. The pleading.

No help came. Breathlessly, she staggered across the room and collapsed on the bench.

"It's so hot," she said. Her voice sounded small and far away. Her heart was pounding in her ears.

"Don't move. No unnecessary exertion," ordered Pres.

Jamie leaned forward and dropped to her

hands and knees, her head hanging down.

"What're you doing?"

"Heat . . . rises," she gasped. "Get down low. Like in a fire."

"This is not a fire," said Pres with sudden fury. "This is a stupid accident. A stupid way to die."

"Die?" *Was that what was going to happen*, she wondered vaguely. *Was she going to die?*

"Any way is a stupid way to die," she said, and giggled as if she'd said something wonderfully funny. She sat down on the floor, feeling the heat of the burning boards against her flesh.

It hurt.

As long as I hurt, I'm still alive, she thought in surprise.

"NOOO!" Pres screamed. He threw himself at the door with all his might. He hammered it with all his might.

But it was in vain. At last he turned, his eyes wild, breath coming in painfully short gasps. Jamie raised her head and tried to focus. She frowned. Why was Pres so far away? With a mighty effort she raised her hand and wiped the sweat from her eyes.

"I never thought I'd die like this," she said in a conversational tone of voice, as if she and Pres were at a party. "Trapped in a room, burned alive. And not even a fire." The thought made her giggle. "Unless I spontaneously combust. Now that would be a fire."

"Stop it!" Pres ordered harshly. "Stop . . . talking . . ."

"Right," she said. "Of course. Don't talk. Save air. Save energy."

Burn quietly.

"I bet this is not as bad as when you burn up in a fire," she heard herself say aloud.

Pres leaned down and lifted her up as if she had weighed nothing at all. He shook her by the shoulders so hard that her head snapped back and forth. "Stop it!" he commanded. "Stop it! Stop saying those things! You're not going to die."

The room spun. She wanted to laugh.

She wanted to cry.

When Pres let her go, her knees wouldn't hold her. She reeled and would have fallen if he hadn't caught her at the last minute and eased her to the floor. Then he staggered to the far wall and slid down onto one of the benches. He rocked forward and buried his face in his hands. "No, no, no," he whispered to himself.

She tried to get up. Tried to walk toward him. Tried to tell him not to worry, that it would be okay.

She fell. The burning wood was against her face now. She closed her eyes and red dots, like burning embers, danced behind her eyelids.

She opened her eyes again,

The light was blinding.

The air was freezing.

Heaven, she thought confusedly. But the angels were too familiar to be real.

"Oh, my god!" shouted Blaine. "Jamie! What are you doing in the sauna?"

"Burning," murmured Jamie.

"Get some water! Get the manager! Call the hotel doctor!" ordered Blaine over her shoulder.

"Pres! Ohmigod, there's Pres!" screamed Alison.

Jamie heard, rather than saw, Pres being led to a bench. She felt cool water touch her lips. She lifted her head and took a gulp and then another. "Thanks," she said, looking up into her cousin's anxious, frightened face.

And then she fainted.

Blaine paced the room like an elegant, angry cat. "You're sure the door wouldn't open?" she demanded.

Jamie, curled in the chair in a corner of the sitting room in Blaine's suite, watched her cousin warily. She'd forgotten this side of Blaine, this frighteningly icy rage. When Blaine was like this, she was unpredictable.

"You're absolutely certain?" Blaine repeated.

"Yes," said Jamie firmly. "Why?"

Blaine turned. Her blue eyes were cold. Cold as winter. Cold as death. "Because when we got there, the door opened easily. I pulled it open with one hand."

"Ask Pres," said Jamie. "You did ask him, didn't you?"

The door opened and Clara slipped noiselessly in. Blaine frowned as Clara crossed the room to the desk by the window. But she only said, "Yes. He agrees with you. The door to the sauna was shut. Tight."

Clara raised her head. "Shouldn't you be resting?" she asked Jamie.

"I've been resting," said Jamie. "I'm tired of resting. I'm not dead, you know. It was just an accident. No one was even hurt."

Blaine suddenly smiled and the icy rage melted from her eyes. "Hear that, Clara? Jamie's fine. Pres is all bent, but Jamie is ready to rock and roll."

"Blaine," said Clara warningly.

But a new, equally dangerous light had appeared in Blaine's eyes. "Tomorrow, I'm marrying Pres," she said. "I'm becoming respectable in the eyes of the world. Tonight, I'm still free. Tonight, let's blow everyone off, Jamie. Let's . . ."

"Blaine. Ms. Harrod. You have a formal dinner tonight," said Clara. "You can't miss that."

Blaine's chin went up and she glared at her assistant.

Clara stood her ground calmly, unmoved by the danger signals.

Blaine turned away first. "You're right," she said tonelessly. "Always right, Clara. What does it feel like to be always right? Jamie, why don't you go get a little more rest. . . . I'll see you tonight."

But as Jamie stood up obediently, Blaine caught her eye.

And gave Jamie a conspiratorial wink. *No one tells me what to do*, the wink said.

"See you around," said Blaine as Jamie left.

And Jamie knew that Blaine wasn't talking about the dinner.

"If you didn't want to come to the party, why didn't you just say so?" asked Drew. "Isn't locking yourself in the sauna with your cousin's fiancé a little extreme?"

Drew slid his arm around Jamie's waist.

She smiled up at him.

"Are you all right?" someone cried, and Stephanie Alden bounced up to join them. "Pres looks *ghastly*! Like he died or something!"

"The hotel doctor said it could have killed us. But no damage was done. We weren't in there long enough to do anything except get scared and hot. And dehydrated," added Jamie, snagging a glass of seltzer and lime from a passing waiter.

Alison murmured, "Such an odd . . . accident."

Stephanie looked at Alison and frowned. Then she said, "It *is* weird, don't you think? All these awful things happening. It's almost like a sign."

"A sign of what?" asked Alison.

Drew said quickly, "Anybody else want anything to drink?"

But he failed to stop Stephanie. "A sign that this wedding isn't meant to be," she said. She looked around at the others. "I mean, come on! You must have thought of it! What other reason could there be? What do you think?"

"I think I see someone I should know," Alison said, and drifted away.

Kelly gave a little hoot of laughter. "Alison is *so* sick," she said.

Stephanie looked as puzzled as Jamie felt. "I don't get it," Stephanie said.

"Kel has a theory that Alison likes to start trouble — and then get out of the way," Drew explained.

"What trouble?" Stephanie's puzzled frown deepened. "You don't think . . . you don't think Alison's the one who's doing the wedding wipeout? Do you?"

"No!" Kelly was indignant. "That wasn't what I meant at all."

"But don't Alison and Blaine, like, hate each other? I mean, aren't they, like, total rivals or something?" Stephanie asked. "Patricia said they were."

Kelly said, "Sure, but half of it's just for publicity, you know. It makes good press. Like that."

"What about the other half?" Stephanie asked slyly.

"You'd have to ask Blaine and Alison about that. But take my advice. Don't get between them in a fight." Kelly paused and added, "Or on a shoot."

"Maybe . . . maybe Alison sabotaged Blaine's wedding for the publicity?" said Stephanie triumphantly.

"Puh-lease," said Kelly, rolling her eyes.

A waiter touched Jamie's elbow lightly. "You're wanted on the hotel phone, miss," he murmured in her ear.

Jamie turned in surprise. "Who is it?" she asked.

"I don't know," said the waiter impassively. "The manager sent me. You'd need to go to the manager's desk and ask him."

"Excuse me," said Jamie to the others. She groaned inwardly. It was probably her mother checking up on her. Asking her if what she'd read in the papers was true.

She threaded her way among the clusters of people, swimming in a sea of heady, expensive perfumes and tantalizing bits of dialogue, carrying on an imaginary conversation with her parents in her head, convincing them that Everything Was All Right.

She stopped. Frowned. Wasn't that Alison, going up the stairs? Who was she with?

Jamie frowned harder as she recognized the man Alison was standing so close to, talking to so intensely.

It was the guy who owned the doves. All the dead doves.

The manager said, "Ms. Haroldson?"

Jamie spun around, startled. "Uh, yes. That's me."

"If you'll go to the first phone booth over

there, I'll transfer the call to you."

When Jamie looked back, Alison and the animal handler were gone.

Jamie slid into the phone booth, remembering her ruse to get the manager away from the desk early that morning. It seemed so far away now. A lifetime ago.

The phone rang.

She picked it up.

"Hello?"

"Jamie?"

Not Mom. Good.

"Who is this?"

"Me, darling. Who else would it be?"

"Blaine? Blaine!"

"Meet me at the side entrance in five minutes, darling. And *don't tell anyone*."

The phone went dead.

Chapter 10

Jamie hung up the phone.

She remembered Blaine's sly wink earlier. What trouble was Blaine planning?

Blaine the wild. Blaine the crazy. Blaine the beautiful.

Jamie smiled suddenly. Did it matter? Whatever happened, it would be interesting.

She slipped across the lobby and walked quickly toward the side entrance. Her hand was on the knob when she sensed someone behind her.

"Who's there?" she said.

No one answered. Tastefully lit, discreetly quiet, the hall was empty.

But Jamie was sure she'd heard something. Felt something. Someone. Watching.

Rose, she thought suddenly. *Here comes the ghost, here comes the ghost . . .*

No. No such thing as ghosts.

"Is anyone there?" she said again, more loudly.

The heavy silence swallowed her words.

Chill, Jamie told herself. *It was just a guest, going to their room. Or someone on the hotel staff.*

Or a murderer.

Shaking off the thought, Jamie resolutely pushed the side exit door open. It closed behind her with a heavy thunk as she stepped out onto the broad, shallow steps.

The moon was half-full, enough light to make the shadows seem darker, the shapes larger and more looming.

"Blaine?" said Jamie, peering into the darkness beyond the light above the entrance.

No one answered. Jamie shivered. The night was chilly and very still, except for the distant thunder of the waves beating on the shore. "Blaine?" she said again, more loudly. She walked down the stairs.

The car came out of nowhere. Jamie didn't have time to move. To even scream.

It missed her by an inch before swerving to a stop on the frozen velvet grass. The door opened.

"Get in," said Blaine's voice with a soft laugh.

"Are you crazy!" Jamie shouted.

Blaine's only answer was another soft laugh.

Jamie got in the car.

She could barely see her cousin's face by the lights from the dashboard. "Blaine, you nearly killed me. You know that?"

"Nope. If I'd wanted to hit you I would have." Blaine patted the leather-padded steering wheel of the gleaming black Porsche affectionately. "This car doesn't make mistakes." She turned to Jamie. "And neither do I."

She accelerated so suddenly that Jamie felt as if she was taking off in a plane. They cut across the black-velvet lawn and bumped onto the stone-paved drive in front of Sandhill.

"I bet you chewed that grass up," said Jamie.

"Oh, dear. I chewed up the perfect grass by the perfect mansion in the perfect world of all the perfect people who deserve to be perfect because they're so rich." Blaine's voice dripped acid.

She turned on the headlights and they swept out down the long driveway. Jamie looked over her shoulder as they roared through the gates.

Sandhill stood alone, a vast fairy-tale castle, lit for the ball. Only Cinderella was leaving the party behind.

They drove in silence, cutting through the

darkness of the narrow, hedge-bound lanes. Jamie didn't ask where they were going. She'd never been in a car like this before. It was enough to be along for the ride.

They roared into the village. The lights of the expensive shops flashed by. The post office. The drug store. The movie theater.

Jamie liked to hang out in the village with her friends. But she'd never been in most of the stores.

Then the village was gone. Now they were winding through the streets of more modest neighborhoods, where the houses were closer to each other and to the road, where the cars parked out front were older and more practical, where the lights from television sets flickered against the drawn curtains of dens with wall-to-wall, stain-resistant carpeting.

"No place like home," Jamie muttered sarcastically, as Blaine slowed down.

When they passed Blaine's house, she slowed down a little more. But she didn't stop. She didn't stop until they reached the pier at the end of town.

In the previous century, it had been the dock where the whaling ships came into harbor from the bay. But tourists had replaced the whales, docking their boats, keeping the concession stands that lined the dock in business during the summer, strolling out to the end of it to take pictures of each other and the view.

But the concession stands were boarded up. The pier was deserted.

Blaine parked her car in the empty lot and got out. She started walking toward the end of the pier.

"Hey, you'll freeze," said Jamie, getting out, too.

Blaine didn't answer.

"Hey, I'll freeze," Jamie added.

"Grab my coat out of the back," Blaine said.

Jamie groped around and a moment later was hurrying after Blaine, wrapped in Blaine's butter-soft leather coat.

"Do you ever miss it?" asked Jamie as she came to a stop by Blaine at the railing at the end of the dock. "Point Harbor, I mean."

"No," said Blaine. "But I never forget it."

The wind picked up slightly for a moment. The water lapped against the pier, the boats rocked, pulling at their ropes and making them creak. The air was sharp, with a faint, fishy odor.

"I've been lucky, you know," said Blaine.

"You've worked hard," said Jamie loyally.

"A lot of people work a lot harder and never get anywhere," said Blaine. She paused, then added, "At least, not anywhere that I'd want to be."

Jamie shivered. "It's cold," she said.

"There's a poem I remember reading," said Blaine, still staring out over the water. "About the world ending in fire or in ice. Which is the worst way to end? To burn? Or to freeze?"

"Right now, I'd vote freeze," said Jamie.

"Fire," said Blaine almost dreamily. "Can you imagine? It must be a little like being trapped in the sauna. Only worse. Don't you think?"

"Blaine, forget the sauna, okay?"

"Fire or ice," said Blaine. "They say it's easy to freeze. Or drown. But not to burn."

"Blaine."

The wind rose to a mournful howl.

Blaine turned. For one moment, Jamie shrank back from the awful flame that seemed to leap up in her cousin's shadowed eyes.

Then Blaine smiled and shivered and was herself again. "Anyway, you're right. It's freezing. *I'm* freezing. Let's get outta here."

But the Porsche wasn't alone in the parking lot anymore. To one side of it, facing in the opposite direction, a Mercedes idled, its engine throbbing with a deep, powerful purr.

"Well, well, well," said a voice from the

passenger window of the Mercedes. "It's the runaway bride."

"Patricia," said Blaine, her voice expressionless. She got into the Porsche. Jamie followed suit, sliding quickly into the passenger seat.

"What are you doing here?" She blurted out.

"I saw Blaine leaving. I followed her. I thought she might be going to a better party."

"You mean one you weren't invited to?" said Blaine smoothly.

For a moment, Patricia's eyes narrowed. But before she could answer, Pres got out of the driver's side of the car. As he did, another voice spoke lazily from the back of the Benz. "Actually, it was me, Blaine. We were a little concerned. You didn't . . . seem yourself. Patricia was with Pres when I found him. She insisted on coming along, too. Wasn't that nice of her?"

"I'll thank you later for interfering in my business, Alison," Blaine said in a cold, hard voice. As she spoke the heavy door of the Mercedes closed with a solid but far from reassuring thud. A moment later, Pres was striding across the parking lot, his handsome face angry.

"What the hell were you thinking of, just

running out of the party like that?" he demanded.

"I needed some fresh air," said Blaine.

"And you couldn't just step outside? You had to drive away and leave me to worry that something had happened to you?"

"I'm a big girl," said Blaine, her voice tight with annoyance. "I can take care of myself. Besides, I had Jamie with me."

Pres ignored Jamie. "Damn it, Blaine, after what's been happening, you can't just leave like that. Suppose something had happened to you!"

"Then you'd be a widower before you were ever a groom," said Blaine.

Pres's hand shot out. His fist slammed into the car.

Jamie flinched, but Blaine never moved. She just sat there, her eyes on Pres.

"What did you say?" asked Pres between gritted teeth.

"Better dead than wed?" said Blaine lightly.

Pres yanked the door of the Porsche open. "Get out of the car," he said.

"No," said Blaine. "And if you keep pushing me, it's the same answer you're going to get at the altar tomorrow, Pres, darling."

Jamie couldn't believe her ears. Was Blaine trying to pick a fight with Pres?

Quickly she reached out and put her hand on Blaine's arm. "Blaine, you're upset. Pres is just worried about you."

"Is he? Is that what it is, Pres? Are you worried about me? Because you love me so much? More than anyone else in the world? More than life itself? Till death do us part?" Blaine's voice was intense, shaking. Her hands on the steering wheel trembled visibly, the knuckles white.

Pres took a deep breath. "Listen to Jamie, Blaine. You're upset. Tired. You're not in any condition to drive. Why don't you get out of the car and come with me? Let me take you back to Sandhill to get some rest." He tried to smile and almost succeeded. "After all, you've got a big day tomorrow. *We've* got a big day tomorrow."

Blaine stared up at Pres. The rigid, strained look gradually left her face. "I am tired," she said softly. "So tired." She slid out of the car to face Pres. "You do love me, don't you?" she asked.

"Of course I do," said Pres, sliding his arm around her shoulders and guiding her back to the car.

"And you'd never, ever lie to me, would you?" asked Blaine, her voice sounding almost like a little girl's. "I can trust you."

At the last moment he half-turned. "Can you find your way back?" he asked Jamie over his shoulder.

"Yes, of course. But . . ."

"But what?" asked Pres impatiently.

Jamie blushed in the darkness. "I don't know how to drive Blaine's car."

A snort of laughter sounded from the back-seat of the Mercedes. "I do," said Alison. She got out and walked over to the Porsche. "Outta the car, junior," she said.

"What?" Jamie was outraged.

"You heard me," said Alison. "I don't mind driving this very nice toy of Blaine's back to Sandhill. But I'm not chauffeuring the children."

Jamie's eyes blazed. "Fine!" she snapped. She jumped out of the car and slammed the door so hard the window rattled.

She heard Alison's mocking laugh as she stalked over to the Mercedes and slid into the backseat.

The Porsche roared to life and swept out of the parking lot.

They followed at a more leisurely pace.

If Blaine drove fast, Alison drove like a bat out of hell. In no time at all, the taillights of the Porsche had shrunk to tiny red specks in front of them, flickering in and out as it went around the curves.

No one in the car spoke. Blaine, who had taken Patricia's place in the seat next to Pres, leaned her head wearily against the seat, one hand resting lightly on Pres's leg.

Patricia stared out the window, pointedly ignoring Jamie.

Suddenly Pres said, "She'd better slow down. There's a bad curve up ahead. And this is the sea-cliff road."

Blaine raised her head.

Pres drew a sharp breath. "I don't believe this. She's not even putting on the brakes."

Ahead of them, the car veered wildly.

"It looks like she's lost control," Jamie gasped.

The small black car leaped across the dividing line, then fishtailed back.

"Put on the brakes, *put on the brakes!*" screamed Blaine.

The car shot out to the edge of the road. It seemed to teeter there for an eternity. Then Alison regained control and rounded the bend in the road on a screech of two tires.

The Benz leaped forward in pursuit.

But it was too late. They rounded the curve just in time to see Blaine's Porsche make a perfect arc into the air, then drop down the hill beside the curve.

Pres braked to a stop. Jamie was out and running before he even turned the motor off. She ran to the edge of the cliff amid the screaming of metal against stone. She saw the lights of the Porsche sweep across the dark landscape like a crazy spotlight as the car turned over and over and over.

She smelled the gasoline

She heard Blaine begin to scream.

Then the car burst into flames.

Chapter 11

"No, no, no! Save her! Help her!" Blaine raced past Jamie to the edge of the cliff.

"Blaine, stop!"

Blaine ignored Jamie. She teetered on the cliff's edge. For one awful moment, Jamie thought her cousin would go over.

Then Pres was there, as he always seemed to be, grabbing her arm, pulling her back to safety.

She fought him like a madwoman.

"She's dying!" screamed Blaine, hitting him, struggling to free herself. "Help her! You can't just stand there and watch her die!"

"Don't look," said Pres. "Don't think about it. You can't help her."

"No one can save her now," whispered Jamie.

Below the car burned hotly, brightly, a beautiful, fatal fallen star.

Behind them, Jamie heard the sound of sirens.

Too late. Much, much too late.

Sometime early that morning, they made their way back to Sandhill. Pres drove slowly, staring rigidly ahead. Blaine slumped against the door, her cheek on the cold glass.

"We should have tried to save her," she said softly, over and over. "Why did you stop me? Why didn't you help me?"

Pres didn't answer. He gripped the wheel and tightened his jaw and drove.

Patricia said, "Blaine, listen. The police said it looked as if she died on impact. She didn't feel anything. And you couldn't have saved her. Pres couldn't have. Nobody could have." For once Patricia sounded almost human.

"We didn't know that then," said Blaine.

"I don't understand why she didn't slow down," Patricia said, pursuing her own thoughts. "They said there weren't even any skid marks. And we didn't see her brake lights, either. It was almost as if . . ."

"As if what?" asked Jamie.

Pres said, roughly, "It was an accident, okay! A tragedy. These things happen."

They'd reached Sandhill. Although it was very late, a flurry of activity met them: the doorman opening the door; Clara urging Blaine out of the car, murmuring soothing words; the night manager of the hotel, speaking in low, earnest tones to Pres.

Jamie got out. She'd been there less than two days. But it seemed a lifetime.

"Jamie! Are you all right?" It was Drew, dark circles of fatigue under his eyes.

"What are you doing up?" asked Jamie. As she spoke a huge yawn threatened to overwhelm her.

"We heard what happened. I wanted to make sure you were okay."

Patricia got out to stand beside Jamie and Drew. "Touching," she murmured.

"I'll walk you guys to your rooms," offered Drew.

"I can find my own way, thanks," said Patricia. Jamie turned. Patricia's eyes were on Pres as, pale and obviously maintaining rigid self-control, he nodded a dismissal to the night manager and strode into the hotel after Blaine and Clara.

Patricia, out of all of them, had been curiously unmoved by the accident. She'd been the one who'd called the police on the car phone when everyone else had leaped out. Only after the police arrived had she gotten out of the car. She'd never gone to the edge of the cliff to look over, never even, as far as Jamie could remember, looked in that direction.

Maybe she wasn't human. Maybe this was her normal state. Ice cold. No feelings at all.

Unless you counted the obsessive, chilling rage in her eyes now as she watched Pres disappear.

Jamie reached out and touched Patricia's arm. "Patricia?"

"What?"

"In the car just now. You said the police found no skid marks. That we didn't see any brake lights. That it was almost as if — as if what, Patricia?"

Patricia continued to stare after Pres. Her voice was flat, matter-of-fact, almost detached. "As if it wasn't an accident. As if Alison wanted to die." She paused as Jamie drew in a sharp breath.

"After all," Patricia concluded, "Alison loved Pres once, too, you know. What better revenge than to kill yourself in front of the guy who dumped you, the night before his wedding? It's the perfect wedding gift, don't you agree?"

"It's sick!" cried Jamie.

"I wish I'd thought of it myself," answered Patricia.

"It's not true," Jamie said numbly as Drew unlocked the door of her room. "You don't believe what Patricia said, do you?"

"Why would anybody believe anything Patricia said?" asked Drew.

Wearily Jamie turned on the light. "Alison wasn't like that," she said. "I didn't know her that well, but I don't believe she'd ever do something like that."

"No. Patricia's taking an awful accident and making it worse," agreed Drew. "The best thing to do is to ignore what she said. Forget it. Consider the source. And try to prevent her from blabbing it around."

Jamie stopped, stricken with guilt. "Oh, Drew. Kelly! I forgot. How is she . . . ?"

Drew said, "She took it hard. The hotel doctor gave her something to help her sleep."

"I'll go see her in the morning first thing, before we have to start getting ready for the wedding . . ."

Jamie's voice trailed off. "It is morning already, isn't it? But is there going to be a wedding?"

Drew leaned forward and kissed Jamie

lightly on the forehead. "Clara will let you know. Go to sleep. Try to get some rest."

Who could sleep? Jamie thought. She'd never been so tired in her whole life. But her nerves jumped like hot wires beneath her skin. Her brain seethed with images: roses and smoke, the ghostly bride reaching out from the mirror, standing above the ballroom, the hot, pulsing walls of the sauna, the car that had become Alison's funeral pyre. . . .

She closed her eyes. But she wasn't asleep.

She wondered if any other members of the wedding were.

Kelly didn't sleep. She'd flushed the pill the doctor had given her. She hadn't needed it. Hadn't wanted it.

But as the grieving best friend she'd been obliged to take it.

She didn't want to sleep. Maybe she'd never sleep again. The accident had inspired her. Given her new, manic energy. She wanted to be alert. Awake. Blaine's wedding was going very, very wrong.

She wanted to be ready for what happened next.

* * *

"She's sleeping," Clara told Pres, kindly but firmly, when he tapped lightly on the door to Blaine's suite.

"I can't," said Pres. "I . . . can't."

"Do you want to discuss calling off the wedding when Blaine wakes up?" asked Clara. "Is that it?"

"No! No, we can't." Pres forced a smile. "I think we should go on. I think Alison would have wanted us to."

Clara didn't say anything.

Pres rubbed his eyes with his hands. "It's just that . . . it was so awful. And everything that has happened . . ."

"It will be all right," said Clara, reaching out to touch his arm. But she stopped herself. She was an employee. It wasn't her place. "You'll be married soon and then it will all be over."

Blaine listened to them talk from the other side of the slightly open door. Pres, suffering. Clara, cold, professional, efficient.

Like a nurse, almost.

Blaine smiled to herself, but her hands were shaking.

Relax, she told herself. The wedding will go on. The show will go on.

Her smile turned bitter. *You have everything you want,* she thought. *Everything you need.*

Except maybe the perfect wedding.

The smell of smoke made her turn her head. Her eyes widened. "You!" she gasped. "No! What are you doing here. . . ."

This wouldn't have happened if he'd married me, like he was supposed to, thought Patricia. She was sitting at her mirror, brushing her hair a hundred strokes, just as her mother did.

No matter what happened, her mother always brushed her own hair a hundred strokes before she went to bed.

Patricia did too. She watched herself in the mirror as she brushed.

I'm glad I don't look like Blaine Harrod," she thought. "She's so flashy. Tacky. Trashy."

Stroke, stroke, stroke. So soothing. So . . . sensual, somehow.

Pres had always admired her hair. Had liked to touch it. She imagined him standing behind her someday, brushing it, her eyes meeting his in the mirror. She'd smile. He'd put the brush slowly down. . . .

But Pres was marrying Blaine.

Or maybe he wasn't.

A lot could happen. A lot already had.

She smiled. Stroke. Stroke. Stroke.

* * *

Stephanie was asleep. Her breathing was deep and even. She hardly moved. Her dreams were easy ones.

She slept the sleep of the young. The naive. The innocent.

Or of the profoundly guilty, who have no conscience at all.

Chapter 12

The masses of flowers filling the sitting room of Blaine's suite reminded Jamie of a funeral as she followed Clara to Blaine's bedroom.

When Clara opened the door Blaine jumped and spun around. Her face was white and set. She was wearing a bathrobe of ivory silk and her hair was spilling around her shoulders.

"It's just me," Jamie said. "I came to see how you're doing."

"Fine," said Blaine. She spoke firmly, as if by saying it, she could make it so.

"Are you sure you should go through with this?" Jamie said.

"Yes." Blaine turned and walked over to the dressing table and sat down. She began to put on her makeup. Her hands were not quite steady, but as Jamie watched, the dark circles beneath Blaine's eyes disappeared, color returned to her cheeks.

"Proper makeup is an art of lying," said Blaine. "Don't I look like the beautiful, blushing bride?"

"You look beautiful," Jamie said truthfully.

She wondered if Kelly was faring any better.

A moment later she had her answer.

"Clara let me in," said Kelly tonelessly, stopping in the door of Blaine's room. She was wearing her jeans and an old gray sweater. She folded her arms and hunched her shoulders as if she was in pain. "She said there was no news. I can't believe she's dead. I can't believe you're still going through with this. How can you be so calm?"

"I'm not calm," retorted Blaine. "I'm in control. There's a difference."

Blaine's eyes met Kelly's in the mirror for a long moment. Suddenly she jumped up and ran to her and put her arms around her. "Oh, Kel. I'm so sorry. I can't believe it, either."

"You saw it. Did she . . . did it hurt?"

"No," said Blaine quickly, before Jamie could answer. "The car went out of control for some reason and over the cliff. Just like that. She didn't even have time to be scared."

"Just mad as hell," said Kelly, her eyes suddenly wet. "I bet she was giving that car a piece of her mind when . . . it happened."

Blaine managed a smile and said, "I bet you're right."

"You could postpone it, you know," said Kelly.

Blaine dropped her arms. She turned back to the makeup mirror and stared at her reflection again. "I could. But I'm not. And you're not quitting on me, either. Are you?"

"N-no," said Kelly slowly. "I guess not."

"Mr. Alden . . ." said Clara, opening the door. She was holding a bouquet of flowers and a package.

"NO!" shrieked Blaine, slamming a compact down on the table. "No, don't let him in. I *told* you, Clara. It's bad luck for the groom to see the bride before the ceremony. . . ." Blaine's voice trailed off as if she realized how idiotic the old superstition was now. What else could happen?

"So much for calm," she muttered. She paused, then said deliberately, "Sorry, Clara. Is Pres out there?" She stood up and walked toward Clara, tightening the sash of her robe.

"Darling, take it easy. I'm not coming in," said Pres's voice from beyond the door. "I know the rules."

"Mr. Alden sent you these. And this came, too." Clara held out the flowers and the package.

Mechanically Blaine took them. "Lovely," she said. "And with a Waterford crystal vase. Nice touch." She took the flowers to the table by the window and set the vase down carefully. She stood for a long moment, her fingers stroking the leaves, her eyes focused on the scene outside.

"So, Clara, are the reporters at the gates? Is there lots and lots of vulgar publicity, the kind that the Alden family hates?"

"No one has been admitted to the grounds of Sandhill except registered guests," said Clara.

"I hate it, too, Clara. You believe me, don't you?"

Clara didn't answer.

Jamie thought, with a sudden, sickening lurch of her stomach, *Is that why Blaine is going on with the wedding? Is it for the publicity? Had Alison, by bitter irony, managed to give Blaine's wedding a publicity boost that would send it off the charts?*

Restlessly, Blaine picked up the flat, silver-wrapped package that had come with the flowers. She tore off the silver paper and let it drop to the floor. "Have you heard anything else, Clara? About the . . . the accident?"

Clara cleared her throat.

Blaine frowned down at the silver frame. She turned it around in her hands. Her eyes widened.

Before Clara could answer, Blaine flung the picture down. She turned and swept the flowers from the table. The vase smashed into a million pieces and water, glass, and broken flowers were scattered across the floor.

"Noo!" sobbed Blaine. She turned, flailing like a madwoman out of control. She grabbed a lamp and hurled it against the far wall of the bedroom. She pushed over the table it was standing on.

Kelly froze, her mouth open. Jamie leaped forward and then ducked as Blaine tore a painting from the wall and threw it blindly.

"Blaine, stop!" Jamie shouted.

But Blaine kept screaming, a wail that was no human word, just an endless sound of anguish.

Then Pres was there. He grabbed her arms and pulled her to him.

Blaine arched her back and tried to pull away. "You sent it!" she cried. "Don't touch me! It was you! How could you!"

"You didn't like the flowers? I promise never to send you flowers again," said Pres, trying to soothe her. "It's all right," he said. "It's okay." His arms closed around Blaine's slender body like iron, holding her tightly, forcing her to stand still.

"The picture!" she panted. "You sent it! If you didn't want to marry me, why didn't you say so? Just tell me that you have another wife somewhere or . . ."

"Stop it!" Pres ordered, in an almost inhuman voice.

Blaine froze. Then suddenly she went limp against Pres and rested her head against his chest, her body trembling, silent tears running down her cheeks.

Clara said, "I'll get some water."

"What happened?" asked Pres, his voice still harsh. "What's she talking about?"

"This, I think. It came with your flowers." Kelly leaned over and picked up the silver-framed picture. She stared down at it curiously. Then her expression changed to one of horror and disgust. "Oh, my god," she whispered. "Oh, my god."

"What?" Jamie looked over Kelly's shoulder.

She felt a chill to the bone.

Kelly was holding the famous photograph of the bride and bridesmaid scene that Blaine and Alison had done together. The one that had, supposedly, been the cause of their feud.

In it, the bride leaned forward, her lips parted, her face feral and beautiful, her hands on the silver letter opener. The bridesmaid, equally beautiful, equally dangerous-looking, sat, looking down at the letter opener that had been stuck in the table between her outstretched fingers.

Blaine and Alison. Alison and Blaine.

The picture had been carefully cut from the magazine and carefully slipped inside the frame.

Which made what had been done to the picture all the more horrifying somehow.

Because the figure of Blaine in the picture had been carefully singed and scorched and turned almost to ash. And beneath it, in heavy, black, block letters were printed the words:

IT SHOULD HAVE BEEN YOU.

"Let me see," said Pres.

Wordlessly Kelly handed the silver-framed picture to him.

He looked down at it. His face grew pale. His grip tightened on Blaine. But all he said was, "I never sent this. How could you think I would, Blaine?"

"It came with the flowers," said Blaine. "The flowers were from you."

"It was on the floor outside your door," said Pres. "I picked it up and handed it to Clara with the flowers."

Clara returned with a glass of water.

"You should lie down," Pres said to Blaine. But Blaine pulled away.

"I'm fine," Blaine insisted, almost angrily. "I'm fine."

Blaine took the picture out of Pres's hand. She examined it for a long moment.

Then she handed it back to Pres. "If you'll excuse me," she said. "I've a wedding I'm supposed to attend."

Pres's face was expressionless. He didn't look down at the picture again. Instead, he studied Blaine's face.

"Are you sure?"

"Are you?" she challenged him. "Or have you changed your mind?"

Suddenly she put her hand on his chest, over his heart. Almost mechanically, his hand came up to cover hers. "We could leave it all now," she said urgently. "Dump the wedding. Run away and get married secretly and . . ."

"NO!" Pres almost shouted, paler than ever.

"You're hurting me," said Blaine in the surprised voice of a child, looking down at her hand beneath Pres's.

"Sorry." Pres released her hand and stepped back.

"I'll see to it that the police get this," he said at last, struggling to maintain his calm.

"Do that," said Blaine. "Clara, could you help me restore some order in here?"

Clara said, "Certainly." To Pres she said, "You could give it to the police now. They're here."

"At Sandhill? Now?" Blaine asked sharply. Then she said, "Oh. The extra security for the wedding."

"Not exactly," said Clara. "It's a detective."

"A detective!" exclaimed Blaine.

"It seems they have some further questions," Clara went on. "It seems they want to know about the accident. But they've agreed to wait until after the wedding."

"How generous of them," said Blaine softly, her eyes on Clara's face. "But go on, Clara. I can tell by your complete lack of animation that there's even more to this fascinating story."

Clara said woodenly, "They think that Alison's accident . . . apparently wasn't one. It looks as if someone had tampered with the brakes of the car."

"So it's true," Blaine said. "Bride flambé, that's what I was supposed to be. The fried bride. Maybe it's an old flame of yours, Pres.

Get it? That's a joke. An old flame . . ."

"Stop it! Stop it *now*!" Pres roared.

Jamie shrank back instinctively at the rage in Pres's face.

Blaine didn't move. She looked up into his eyes with a little, sad smile. Her voice had become the voice of a little girl again. "But you won't let them, will you? You'll protect me. You won't let anyone hurt me."

"No," said Pres.

"You promise?" said Blaine.

Pres leaned over and pulled Blaine to him hard. He kissed her roughly. Then he almost pushed her away. His jaw was set, his face grim.

"I promise," he said.

He stepped back. He looked around the room but Jamie had a feeling he wasn't really seeing any of them.

He said, "Don't you have a wedding to get ready for?"

Blaine laughed. "Oh, I'll be ready. I'll be there. After all, you can't start the wedding without the bride."

The knock on the door made Jamie jump.

She hurried across and unlocked it.

"Let me in!" Kelly gasped, practically falling into the room. Over her shoulder, she said,

"Bring those in and put them, oh, anywhere. I don't care."

A hotel porter came staggering through the door carrying dress bags and suitcases and makeup kits. When he'd put them down, Kelly gave him a tip and waved him away.

"Kelly, what are you doing?" said Jamie.

"I'm getting ready in here. I hate my room. Everywhere I look, I see things that Alison left lying around. She was such a slob. You wouldn't believe it, would you, because she was so down, so pulled together. It was her dark secret," Kelly rattled on at top speed. "So can I get ready in here? I mean, like if this hotel isn't haunted already, it will be. I'm outta here, right after the ceremony, I promise you . . ."

"Kel, chill. Of course you can get ready in here." Jamie was more glad of Kelly's company than she cared to admit.

Kelly kept talking. She talked about modeling. About her family. About Pres and Blaine. About Alison.

"Alison and Blaine started out together, you know? They had this, like, tiny, minuscule apartment in this totally uncool part of Manhattan, you know? They shared it with another model who didn't make it and just sort of gave up and disappeared or something. But they didn't give up. Alison hit first, you know. But Blaine was right behind her. And then I came along and you know what? They were really decent to me. I mean, Alison seems cold and I know Blaine is made of, like, iron? But they have hearts, both of them."

Jamie said, "I'm going to take a quick shower."

The hot water felt good. She wanted to stay in the shower forever. She leaned back to let the water beat against her skin — and the heat of the tiles against her flesh reminded her of the glowing, burning heat of the sauna.

Of the molten, flaming funeral pyre that Blaine's car had become.

She finished her shower quickly.

Kelly had put on her dress and was sitting at the makeup mirror with a towel over her shoulders, studying her face in the mirror. "Shh!" she said as Jamie walked back into the room. "I can't put on makeup and talk at the same time."

Hiding a smile, Jamie began to get dressed for the wedding.

"So Alison and Blaine are friends?"

"Uh-huh. Tighter than you'd think. They have this, like, love-hate relationship. Like sisters or something, you know? Like when Alison started going out with Pres, Blaine was disgusted. Then Pres started dating Blaine and Alison went ballistic. But they worked it out. 'Course they both have real strong personalities . . ."

Kelly *could* put on makeup and talk at the same time, Jamie noted wryly. And her famous model's face was emerging from the mirror.

"So Pres is a heartbreaker?" Jamie said. "Like I didn't know."

"He likes models," said Kelly simply. "I wanted to go out with him myself, you know? But then he met Blaine." She shrugged. "Like his family hates the whole scene, you know? They had ancestors or something that came over with the pilgrims? To them, anybody who really works for a living is trash."

Jamie shimmied into her dress. She glanced at her shoes and decided to wait until the last minute to put them on. They'd seemed glamorous and seductive when she'd bought them. But high heels also meant pain, and Jamie had long ago decided she could be more glamorous and seductive when she wasn't in pain.

But she'd paid a lot for those shoes. She had to wear them sometime. . . .

"Done," said Kelly triumphantly. She motioned to Jamie. "Your turn."

Jamie sat down obediently. It was soothing to let someone else do the work. She let herself drift along on the tide of Kelly's nervous chatter, trying to make her mind blank, trying not to think of everything that had happened.

Of everything that could happen.

"Done!" said Kelly triumphantly at last.

Jamie opened her eyes.

A stranger stared back at her. Mysterious. Older. Dangerous. *Drew would like it,* she thought.

Drew.

Get grounded, Jamie, she told herself. *What you're wearing is a costume. It isn't the real you. This is a dress-up party. Tomorrow it'll all be over.*

Too bad about Drew. She'd have a good time and forget about him when it was over.

"Fabulous, darling," Jamie said aloud to Kelly.

Kelly beamed. For a moment she looked like the kid, not Jamie. For a moment the sadness and fear dropped away. "Yes," she said. "I know."

Patricia's mother didn't believe in makeup, except in the barest, almost invisible amounts. Real ladies didn't wear a lot of makeup.

But then, Pres hadn't proposed to a real lady, had he?

Patricia applied her makeup carefully. It was

only after she'd finished that she realized she should have put her dress on first. What if she smeared it?

She looked at the clock. Not much time left.

She pulled the dress on. But it was her hand, not the dress, that brushed her lipsticked mouth.

The dress in place, she looked down at the crimson gash the lipstick had made across the back of her hand.

At the crimson gash it had made from the corner of her mouth.

"Here comes the bride," she hummed softly, and went back to work on her face.

"Mo-ther, please. Go bother Pres or something," said Stephanie.

Her mother was driving her crazy. She'd been in and out of Stephanie's room at least a hundred times. A million.

Two spots of color appeared on her mother's carefully manicured and maintained face.

Mother dearest will be getting her first face-lift soon, thought Stephanie cruelly. *After all, appearance is everything.*

"It just looks so bad," her mother said fretfully. "All these awful — incidents. And now this. That girl going and getting herself killed right before the wedding."

You don't know the half of it, thought Stephanie. She plopped down in the chair in her room and stretched her legs out. She was ready. She'd been ready for hours. Days. Years.

She'd never had so much fun in her short, spoiled, sheltered life.

"How *can* Pres do this to us," Mrs. Alden went on.

"It's probably hard on Blaine, too," Stephanie said. Not that she was sticking up for Blaine. She just wanted to get on her mother's nerves the way her mother was getting on hers. "After all, Alison was a friend of hers . . . of course, Pres did date her once, too."

Mrs. Alden's mouth set in a thin line. "That's not the point. And I'm sure that creature is reveling in all this publicity. It's in all the papers already. I don't know how they find these things out. Reporters. Vultures!"

"It's almost time for the wedding, Mother," said Stephanie. "You better finish getting ready."

"The only time for this wedding, as far as I'm concerned, is *never*," said Mrs. Alden and left, almost, but not quite, slamming the door behind her.

He walked from one end of the room to the other like a caged animal. A human tiger, pacing, glaring out at his invisible captors.

He was pale. Breathing hard. Sweating.

He hadn't known it was going to come to this. Couldn't believe it was happening. Funny how things got set in motion and then spun out of control.

He hated losing control.

No. No, he wasn't losing control. He could handle this.

He closed his eyes for a moment. Saw the flames. Heard the screams.

He opened his eyes quickly. Don't think about that now. It was over. Done.

It couldn't be helped.

The eyes of the whole world were on this wedding. He had to be calm. To act as if nothing had happened.

He was in control. He could handle it.

From what seemed like far away, he heard the knock on the door.

He turned.

"Time," a voice said. "It's time."

She looked into her mirror and saw another face. A much younger face, even though it hadn't been that many years ago. Only a few years.

Only a lifetime.

So much had happened. Dreams had come true.

Some of them in unexpected ways.

Unpleasant ways.

How had she gotten here?

Be careful what you wish for, she thought. There's no getting out of it now. Don't think about it. Just do it.

That philosophy had served her well. She willed it to work one last time.

She picked up the perfume and sprayed it on recklessly. A heavy, familiar scent clogged the air.

She stood up. She was ready.

A discreet knock sounded on the door. She turned and met Clara's eyes.

"It's time," Clara said.

Blaine walked down the long, long hall. Clara walked a little behind her, helping to hold up the train of the dress. Ahead the doors of the grand ballroom loomed. Blaine could hear the soothing music of the string quartet.

"Here comes the briiide," sang Stephanie delightedly, off-key.

It's like a dream, thought Blaine, walking down the long, long corridor. *So long. So brightly lit.*

She remembered stories she'd read of people who'd almost died. They'd told of going down a long white tunnel. People who'd died before them waited at the end, beckoning them on.

But the bridesmaids were all very much alive.

Except one.

Blaine blinked. For a moment, she'd almost been able to imagine Alison among them.

But it couldn't be.

"You look beautiful," said Kelly. "The prettiest bride in the world."

"You don't look so bad yourself," Blaine managed to say through stiff lips.

She imagined opening the door. She imagined the room filled with flames. The wedding guests burning like bits of paper.

Like . . . no . . . Don't think about it.

Jamie touched her lightly on the arm. Blaine took a sharp breath and tried to smile. It must have succeeded. The worried look left Jamie's face.

Jamie looks like I did, Blaine thought. *Once. Before the end of my innocence.*

Patricia said nothing at all. She just stood there, looking smug, her lips a bright, vampire red.

What did Patricia know? What hold did she have over Pres that he'd insisted she be in the wedding?

Why hadn't it been enough, whatever it was,

for her to insist that he marry her?

Patricia was crazy about Pres, thought Blaine. *Would do anything for him.*

Wouldn't she?

Would she stop at murder . . . ?

She walked forward. "Full house," said Kelly.

"Clara?" said Blaine, in a sudden panic.

Clara was there. "Everything is fine," she said. "Nothing will go wrong." Her eyes held Blaine's for a moment. Steady brown eyes. The eyes of an old friend.

Blaine could trust Clara. Clara would always tell the truth.

She nodded slightly.

The massive doors were flung open.

A moment's pause, and then the wedding march began to play.

Chapter 13

Clara handed out their bridesmaid's bouquets and the young women fell into line: Patricia first now, then Kelly, then Jamie, then Stephanie.

What did Patricia feel, leading the way for the woman who was marrying the man she'd expected to marry?

She looked neither to the right nor left as she walked forward. Her shoulders were rigid, but other than that she seemed unaffected by the event, or by the soft, almost inaudible murmur that swept the onlookers as she walked down the dark-carpeted aisle.

When Patricia was halfway down the aisle, Kelly looked over her shoulder at Jamie. She made a face.

Jamie nodded reassuringly.

Kelly turned, straightened up infinitesimally, and glided forward. The murmur grew louder and more appreciative.

Hardly knowing what she was doing, Jamie started forward. Clara's hand on her arm stopped her at the door. Jamie waited until Kelly was halfway down the aisle.

Then Clara released her and Jamie began the long walk down the aisle.

The room was awash in flowers. Flowers lined the aisle and the altar was a mountain of them. Above the altar, the satin canopy hung, empty this time of doves. Candles burned everywhere, despite the bright light that came from the chandeliers above. The heavy curtains covering the massive windows were closed.

The faces turned up to her like flowers turning toward the sun. Some were curious, some merely interested, some approving and appreciative. She saw Drew. He gave her his best leer and a big wink. She returned it with her best seductive look.

Ahead of her, Kelly stood beside Patricia. The minister stood in the middle, in front of the altar. To the other side stood Pres and his father, who was his best man, and the ushers.

Patricia had a faint, contemptuous smile pinned to her lips. Kelly's smile was tremulous, but genuine. The minister's expression was one of professional wedding joy. The ushers looked handsome and detached and very much like one another in their tuxedos.

Pres's father was stern and unsmiling.

Pres was pale. He didn't move. He stared down the aisle without blinking. His hands were clenched.

How could I be moving so slowly and yet have things go by so fast? Jamie thought. And then she'd arrived. She went to her place beside Kelly and turned.

Stephanie was halfway down the aisle, walking buoyantly rather than gliding. She looked excited, avidly excited. As if she couldn't wait for what would happen next. As if it were all a big adventure, a complete surprise . . .

As if it didn't matter that Alison was dead.

Stephanie landed beside Jamie with a bounce. "Super," she whispered. "Isn't this super!"

"Shhh," Jamie hissed.

"Everybody's looking at the bride," Stephanie whispered back unrepentantly.

It was true. Blaine was a beautiful bride. She seemed to float down the aisle. A small, mysterious smile showed beneath the half-veil that covered her face. The train of her gown spread out like a lacy sea behind her.

Soft *oohs* and *aahs* rose from the guests.

She walked with a stately tread to the altar and Pres stepped forward to stand beside her.

The music swelled and was still.

The minister raised his book. He looked out over his captive audience. He looked down at the bride and groom.

Jamie tensed. If something were going to happen, surely it would be now?

"Dearly beloved," the minister said. The wedding ceremony had begun.

Afterward, Jamie wouldn't remember much about it. She felt as if she were floating above it all, catching fragments of words. She wondered if Blaine felt the same way. So detached.

So out of it.

Or was every sense of Blaine's alert, waiting for something awful to happen . . .

Beside her, Kelly sighed softly. And Stephanie was still, caught up in the moment.

Blaine repeated her words clearly, never missing.

Pres repeated his vows more softly, pausing often, looking around as if for help.

I wonder if he's got cold feet, thought Jamie. *Or if he's just worried about Blaine.*

There was a momentous pause. The minister smiled benevolently down at the couple, now so nearly husband and wife. He looked out over the crowd.

"If anyone should have any reason that this man and this woman should not be joined in marriage, let them speak now . . ."

A tremendous wind seemed to sweep the hall. The vast doors slammed shut. The lights went out and most of the candles were snuffed.

Startled cries and exclamations rose in the near darkness.

"Oh dear!" said the minister. "Stay calm, please. Stay in your seats. We've had this problem before . . ."

His voice trailed off.

The scent of roses filled the room. The scent of roses and of fire.

Then Kelly screamed, "It's her! It's the ghost bride!"

She stood at the back of the room. She was dressed all in white, swathed in a heavy veil. A ghastly glow came from her clothes.

She began to walk down the aisle, slowly, slowly.

The smell of smoke grew stronger.

"I object," she said in a hollow voice.

"Get back!" shouted Pres.

The bride walked on, down the aisle, past the silent, shocked, staring guests.

She stopped to face Pres and Blaine.

"I object," she repeated. "Pres was already married. To me."

"No!" called Pres. He stepped forward, as if to shield Blaine.

The bride laughed.

"So strong. So brave. So true . . ."

"You're dead," gasped Pres. "You can't be, it can't be . . ."

"Dead. Dead because you let me die. You left me there to die. All alone to *dieeee* . . ."

As she spoke the bride threw back her veil. And her dress burst into flames.

Pres lunged forward but stopped. "I couldn't have . . . I had to . . . the scandal . . . I wanted to . . ."

The bride smiled. The flames leaped up around her.

"Save me now," she said. "Kiss me."

"NOOOOO!" screamed Pres. "NO PLEASSSSSE!" And then he was running, running past the burning bride, down the aisle to hammer on the doors. "LET ME OUT! LET ME OUT! IT WASN'T MY FAULT SHE DIED . . ."

The lights came on.

People leaped to their feet. Ushers surrounded Pres, restraining him, holding him back.

"B-Blaine!" gasped Jamie, turning to look at her cousin.

Blaine stood there, beautiful and serene,

looking down at the burning bride.

The flames were dying down. Clara was there, doing something that seemed to be helping.

"Awesome!" shouted Stephanie.

"Oh, Pres, Pres," cried Patricia. She dropped her bouquet on the floor and hurried down the aisle toward her beloved.

And still Blaine stood, looking at the bride.

Clara handed the bride a towel. She reached up and wiped her face and then began peeling it.

Jamie froze.

"AWESOME!" shrieked Stephanie.

Kelly murmured, "Alison? *Alison?*"

And fell to the ground in a dead faint.

Chapter 14

"I don't believe it, I don't believe it! You're alive!"

"I don't think the smoke is ever going to come out of my hair," Alison answered Kelly.

"Forget the smoke. Do you mind telling me *what* is going on?"

"You fainted, Kel."

"That was hours ago. Now tell me everything. I'm about to die of curiosity."

Kelly and Jamie were sitting in Blaine's suite. At Blaine's direction, Jamie and Drew had helped Kelly there after she'd fainted.

And at Blaine's request, they'd stayed.

For hours, it seemed, although not all that long had passed since the lights had come up on the shambles that had been the wedding of the year.

Blaine, coming in behind Alison with Clara, eyed the room service trays heaped up around the suite and said, "At least you're not about to die of starvation."

"I'll order some more coffee and . . ." Clara began.

"Lose the meek assistant role, Clara," said Blaine. "Not that you're not good at it."

Clara smiled. "I'm hungry," she said. "I'm going to order something for *me*. Does anybody else want anything?"

"Answers?" suggested Jamie, her head spinning.

"Coffee first, then answers," drawled Alison.

When the coffee had been served, Alison said, "I think you start the story, Clara."

"Clara!" exclaimed Kelly.

They all looked over at Blaine's meek assistant. But she didn't look so meek anymore. In spite of the flowered, slightly dowdy dress she'd put on for the wedding, in spite of the plain, straight hair, Clara didn't look like Clara at all.

"My name is Clara Dover," she said. "I'm not really Blaine's assistant. In fact, I have degrees in chemistry and physics and I do research for a large environmental firm."

Drew let out a whistle.

"My younger sister, however, had different ambitions, and as soon as she was old enough to leave home, she took off for New York. She wanted to be a model and an actress.

"She got an apartment with two other wannabe models on what could charitably be called the edge of the East Village. She was very young and full of hope and plans. And very, very beautiful.

"At first it was hard. I sent her money when she would let me, as did our parents. But she was proud. She was going to make it on her own. Prove herself.

"She began to have a few successes. To be invited to what she called 'the right parties.' To make 'contacts.'

"The world she was moving into was a jungle. But she and her two roommates had become good friends and they agreed to watch out for each other. 'All for one and one for all, as it were.' "

"Dover," said Kelly suddenly.

Clara looked over at Kelly. "Exactly."

"Exactly what?" cried Jamie.

"Her modeling name was her childhood nickname, which was 'Dove.' " Clara made a small, sad face. "She told me once that she was going to be so famous that all the world was going to know her by that one name.

"At one of the right parties, Dove met a very handsome older man. He'd dated a lot of models and actresses, mostly young, beginning ones. He was from a wealthy old family and they didn't like it. But as long as he wasn't too serious, they could put up with it.

"He fell in love with Dove, I think. Swept off his feet. Became consumed with jealousy every time she even looked at another man. Hated her being a model. Wanted her all to himself.

"He asked her to marry him. She agreed. But he insisted that they get married quietly, that she keep it a secret and tell no one, not even her roommates.

"She didn't. She and he traveled, separately, to a remote island. They checked into separate hotels. Pres picked her up that afternoon in a rental car that he'd gotten, because you can bribe almost anybody to do almost anything if you have enough money, under an assumed name.

"I wonder if he even meant to marry her . . .

"Anyway, they never arrived. Pres lost control of the car and it went over a cliff. Pres was thrown clear, barely scratched.

"Dove was killed.

"Did he try to save her? I don't know. I'll never know. I do know he ran. Ran back to his room. Ran back to his life.

"Left my sister's body to be discovered, burnt almost beyond recognition. It was weeks before they even discovered who she was."

The third roommate, Jamie thought. *That's who Kelly was talking about!*

Blaine said, "Dove had left a note. She was going to be gone a long time. She didn't know when she was coming back. Don't worry, she was happy, she'd never been so happy and we could rent out her room and would we please send all her stuff back home."

"Happy," said Alison. "She'd tell us all about it when she got back. Only she never did come back. We'd had roommates do the disappearing act on us before. At least she'd left her share of the rent. It didn't seem like Dove, but . . ."

"Then we started getting work," said Blaine. "Life got busy. Full. We didn't think about Dove very much, except to miss her. Until Clara contacted me."

"Dove had written me a letter hinting at her marriage. Full of teasing and mystery. Bragging a little, too." Clara smiled wistfully.

"I went down to the island. I retraced her steps. I spoke with many, many people. And at last I came up with something. By some miracle, the hotel where Dove had stayed had saved her things in a box. Some of the things were gone, of course, picked through by the hotel staff. But in the bottom of the box was her journal.

"It told me everything I needed to know. There was even an entry right before Pres picked her up for her wedding. She wrote that she was the happiest girl alive.

"A short time later, she was dead . . .

"I wanted Prescott Alden, rich enough to buy his way out of anything, to pay. To acknowledge what had happened. But his family is powerful and connected. What chance did I stand against them? That's when I thought of making him confess . . ."

Alison said, "I didn't need persuading. He'd just dumped me. And asked my good friend Blaine out."

Blaine shook her head. "All's fair in modeling, but what kind of guy thinks a girl is going to go out with the rat who dumped one of her best friends? But when Clara told Alison and me what had happened, we decided I would go out with Pres. Maybe we could learn something that way.

"Then he asked me to marry him. The rest you know."

"You mean you planned this whole thing?" said Kelly. "This . . . this wedding from hell?"

"Yes." Blaine's lips curved upward. "That's

why I didn't want a flower girl or a ring bearer. This wedding was no place for children!"

"But how?" asked Kelly. "How did you do it all?"

"We planted the ghost rumor with you, Kel," Alison said, her voice taking on its mocking edge. "We knew you'd spread it around."

"The ghost in the mirror?" asked Jamie.

"A trick done with mirrors," said Alison. She smiled. "Sorry. But we knew special effects people and I used to go out with a rather famous magician. If you rig up the lighting, and coordinate the stunt just right, it works every time."

"Thanks a lot," said Jamie. "You nearly scared me out of my wits."

"It was a mistake, actually," said Blaine. "That was supposed to be Pres's room . . ."

"It was the only mistake, though," said Clara calmly. "Everything else went well. Alison did the ghostly bride from the alcove above the small ballroom and then made her getaway in the dark and confusion."

"Asbestos clothes and special effects," said Alison. She made a face. "And I don't ever want to pull burning stunts again, I promise you. It is big-time scary."

"Not as scary as you were," said Kelly.

"But what about the dead doves! You killed them!" cried Jamie.

Alison rolled her eyes. "No. They were stuffed birds. Long time dead. Died of natural causes or something, okay? My friend the magician was the bird handler."

"Oh . . . that explains it. I saw you with him after it happened. You looked like you were having an *intense* conversation, and I wondered . . ." said Jamie.

"Dead doves . . . Dove," murmured Kelly.

Drew said, "I would have confessed right then."

"Pres wasn't a happy bridegroom. He kept trying to persuade me to put the wedding off. But I wouldn't. I kept telling him that I appreciated his concern, but I had to be brave," said Blaine. Her voice was scornful.

"The sauna was another mistake. I had no idea you were in there," said Alison.

"Thanks a lot," said Jamie. "I could have been killed."

Blaine shook her head. "Nope. We just wanted to scare Pres some more, not kill him. And you're being in there did help spread the suspicion around."

"The accident?" asked Kelly. "You rigged that, too."

Alison nodded. "It was easy to make Pres follow Blaine. He's insanely jealous and possessive. But getting that car over the cliff was the trickiest part. Split-second timing. I made myself scarce and Clara picked me up at the prearranged meeting point."

Clara took up the story again. "I suggested that Pres bring Blaine some flowers. I put the package outside the door and waited for him to arrive and find it. Then I took it in with the flowers."

"And the smell of roses?"

"Dove's favorite perfume smelled like that," said Clara. She looked down at her hands, which were tightly clasped on her lap. Slowly she unclasped them. "And that's it."

"So that's it," said Blaine. "Pres completely flipped out. He confessed. And whatever he is or isn't charged with, the whole world knows the story of how Dove died now. He didn't get away with it after all. . . ."

She made a face. "Of course, the whole world has been keeping up to date on my wedding ever since I arrived here. I don't know where the leaks are coming from . . ."

"But darling! All the lovely publicity," Alison murmured.

"You know what you can do with your publicity?" asked Blaine.

A knock sounded on the door.

Drew jumped up and opened it. Stephanie stood there, dressed in jeans and a sweater. Her eyes were downcast. "I just wanted to tell you I'm sorry," she said.

Clara said, "It's not your fault, Stephanie. What Pres did was . . ."

"Not about that!" Stephanie raised her huge eyes. "I'm sorry for what I did!"

Chapter 15

"Did?" said Clara blankly. "What did you do?"

"It was me!" Stephanie wailed. "I was the unnamed source. I kept telling the newspapers what was happening!"

Blaine's mouth dropped open. "You? Why?"

"For fun. This is the most exciting thing that has ever happened to me in my life. I mean, Pres gets to go do anything he wants . . ."

"Not anymore," whispered Kelly to Jamie.

"But you wouldn't believe what a short chain my mother keeps me on."

She went on, "I won't grow up to be some old rich man's face-lifted wife who doesn't do anything, I won't, I won't!"

"You don't have to," said Blaine soothingly. "Knowing you, I'm sure you'll think of a way out."

"Really?" Stephanie looked pleased. "You really think so?"

"I know it," said Blaine firmly, giving Stephanie a little push out the door.

Stephanie went. She stopped on the threshold to say, "I'm so glad you're not mad at me." Then she added, "I'm sorry about what Pres did. He was always a pig brother, though. He fooled Mother and Daddy, but he didn't fool me. I'm glad he got in trouble."

Her cheeks suddenly dimpled mischievously. "And you know what? He's going to end up with Patricia and he's going to deserve that, too!"

With that she was gone.

Blaine closed the door and leaned against it. "Do you believe it?" she asked. And then she started to laugh.

In a minute, Clara joined in. Then Jamie and Kelly and Drew.

They laughed for a long time. Hard. Until their sides ached and they couldn't breathe. Until they cried, some of them.

At last, Clara stopped, wiping her eyes. "It's over," she said wonderingly. "Whatever the consequences, it's over. Dove can rest in peace."

"Yes," said Blaine.

Clara smiled. Then she stood up briskly. "More coffee, anyone?"

Kelly said to Alison, "I could kill you, you

know that? You scared me out of my mind."

Alison said, "Your tiny little mind will survive."

Drew stood up and caught Jamie's hand and pulled her up, too.

"If you'll excuse us," he said. "We've got places to go and things to do."

"I'll bet you do," said Alison. Kelly socked Alison in the arm.

Jamie felt her face turn red.

Blaine said, "Go. But don't go too far."

Alison hooted. Jamie gave her a look. Alison didn't scare her anymore.

"You know," said Blaine, "I didn't mean that the way it sounded. I meant, come back soon. Now that this wedding is over, we've got some catching up to do."

Jamie smiled. "I'll be back."

She followed Drew out into the corridor. "C'mon," said Drew. "We'll get my car and we'll get out of here. I think you need to show me around your part of the world, if I'm going to be coming back this way."

Jamie looked up into Drew's eyes. "Oh, yeah?" she asked.

"Yeah," said Drew. "After all, the wedding's over. But the party has just begun . . ."

About the Author

D. E. Athkins was born and raised in the haunted South, and spent a wasted childhood trying to catch Santa Claus, the Easter Bunny, the Tooth Fairy, and the ghost in a women's dormitory at a local Methodist college. Upon reaching adulthood, Athkins moved to the prosaic North and eventually took up horror writing as a way to fill the gap left by a dearth of supernatural beings.

The author enjoys reading true-crime accounts, criminal case law, murder mysteries, and mail-order catalogs. Athkins will not go to scary movies, is afraid of blood, and believes that there is much more to this world than meets the eye. (What else are cats looking for all the time?) In free moments, Athkins enjoys horrorticulture — accumulating, by fair means or foul, plants for a horror garden at the edge of the woods behind the author's house, where baby's breath and deadly nightshade thrive.

Every day *Sara Howell* faces mystery, danger ... and silence.

Sara Howell is smart, savvy, beautiful ... and deaf.

For Sara and the people of Radley, things get frightening when five people die in the collapse of the Shadow Point Bridge. Then Sara's father is killed in a hit-and-run accident.

Now someone's following Sara. She must find some answers, or she could be the next victim.

HEAR NO EVIL
Death in the Afternoon #1
by Kate Chester

Coming to a bookstore near you.

HNE1195

THRILLERS

D.E. Athkins
☐ MC45246-0 Mirror, Mirror $3.50

A. Bates
☐ MC45829-9 The Dead Game $3.99
☐ MC43291-5 Final Exam $3.50
☐ MC44582-0 Mother's Helper $3.99
☐ MC44238-4 Party Line $3.99

Caroline B. Cooney
☐ MC44316-X The Cheerleader $3.50
☐ MC43806-9 The Fog $3.50
☐ MC45681-4 Freeze Tag $3.99
☐ MC45402-1 The Perfume $3.50
☐ MC44884-6 The Return of
the Vampire $3.50
☐ MC41640-5 The Snow $2.75
☐ MC45680-6 The Stranger $3.50
☐ MC45682-2 The Vampire's
Promise $3.50

Richie Tankersley Cusick
☐ MC43115-3 April Fools $3.50

☐ MC43203-6 The Lifeguard $3.50
☐ MC43114-5 Teacher's Pet $3.50
☐ MC44235-X Trick or Treat $3.50

Carol Ellis
☐ MC44768-8 My Secret Admirer .$3.50
☐ MC44916-8 The Window $3.50

Lael Littke
☐ MC44237-6 Prom Dress $3.50

Christopher Pike
☐ MC43014-9 Slumber Party $3.50
☐ MC44256-2 Weekend $3.99

Edited by T. Pines
☐ MC45256-8 Thirteen $3.99

Sinclair Smith
☐ MC46126-5 Dream Date $3.99
☐ MC45063-8 The Waitress $3.99

Available wherever you buy books, or use this order form.